Jack Yeovil is the ha⋯⋯⋯⋯⋯⋯⋯⋯⋯⋯⋯ de
plume of soft-spoken, white wine-sipping Kim Newman.
As Yeovil, Newman has written a series of fantasy novels
set in the 'Warhammer' universe, while under his own
name he has published the definitive critical guide,
Nightmare Movies and five highly acclaimed novels:
The Night Mayor, Bad Dreams, Jago, Anno Dracula,
and *The Quorum*. His short stories have been widely
anthologised and have been collected in two volumes:
The Original Dr Shade, published in 1994, and *Famous
Monsters* to be published in 1995. Kim and Jack both live
in north London.

By the same author

as **Jack Yeovil**
Drachenfels
Demon Download
Krokodil Tears
Comeback Tour
Beasts in Velvet
Genevieve Undead

as **Kim Newman**
Nightmare Movies
Ghastly Beyond Belief (with Neil Gaiman)
Horror: 100 Best Books (with Stephen Jones)
The Night Mayor
Bad Dreams
Wild West Movies
Jago
Anno Dracula
The Quorum
The Original Dr Shade

JACK YEOVIL

Orgy of the Blood Parasites

POCKET
BOOKS

LONDON · SYDNEY · NEW YORK · TOKYO · SINGAPORE · TORONTO

First published in Great Britain by Pocket Books, 1994
An imprint of Simon & Schuster Ltd
A Paramount Communications Company

Copyright © Kim Newman, 1994

The right of Kim Newman to be identified as author of this work
has been asserted in accordance with sections 77 and 78 of the
Copyright, Designs and Patents Act, 1988.

Simon & Schuster Ltd
West Garden Place
Kendal Street
London W2 2AQ

Simon & Schuster of Australia Pty Ltd
Sydney

A CIP catalogue record for this book is available from the
British Library

ISBN 0-671-85109-8

Printed in Great Britain by HarperCollins*Manufacturing*, Glasgow

'Perhaps some diseases perceived as diseases which destroy a well-functioning machine, in fact change the machine into a machine that does something else, and we have to figure out what it is that the machine now does. Instead of having a defective machine, we have a nicely-functioning machine that just has a different purpose. Part of it is a self-deceptive way of coping with the possibilities of disease, but on the other hand I can imagine what it feels like to be a virus. The AIDS virus: look at it from his point of view – very vital, very excited, really having a good time. It's made the front page, and is really flexing its muscles and doing what it does. It's really a triumph, if you're a virus. It's really good stuff that's happening, it's not bad at all.'

David Cronenberg

'Look . . . look at the audience . . . they've got . . . *wabbititis*!'

Elmer Fudd

Contents

PROLOGUE

Lunacy in the Age of Reason

Oh God oh God oh God oh God . . .

There are no atheists during finals, Pete thought as he evened up the sheet of A4 in his battered manual typewriter. He supposed he was ready to hammer this last exam into the ground on his own abilities, but Divine Intervention might come in handy.

Earth to God, Earth to God!

Soften the hearts of thy Holy Assessors, and let them look with favour upon these the works of thy devoted servant.

Pete flexed his fingers in the air over the keyboard. He reached into himself for that moment of *zen* calm, and was poised to pounce . . .

Upstairs, a Heavy Metal riff started. The ceiling began to vibrate with the thudding bass. Shit! Ten o'clock in the morning! What a time for the Dickhead Twins to start jiving to their record collection!

Lunacy in the Age of Reasonn, he typed, *by Peter Aston*. He rolled the page up and saw the error. He knew he was out of Tippex, but still felt he had to look through his desk drawer.

Oh Lord, grant unto me liquid paper and I shalt sin no more . . .

'I couldn't work, and I couldn't think,
I couldn't face the day until I had another drink,
I asked my doctor, what could I do?
He said, "Son, Deep Depression got a hold on you . . ."'

The intro filled the room. 'Shut the *fuck* up!' he shouted, knowing he had no chance of being heard

13

through the rhythm 'n' racket fuzz-tone guitar. 'Some people are trying to work!'

He pulled the paper out, tearing off a jagged triangle. He crumpled both pieces into a ball, and tore the ball into shreds for good measure. The shreds went into his waste-bin, with the rest of his false starts.

> 'Sometimes it's lack of mon-eeeeee,
> Or maybe lack of friends,
> But ya know Deep Depression
> Gonna getcha in the end!
> I heard my doctor talkin',
> And he weren't bein' vague,
> He say Deep Depression
> Is worse than the PLAGUE!'

Didn't they know it was finals time? Didn't they realize that he had to have three copies of this damn essay on the dean's desk by four-thirty this afternoon or face a *viva voce* Inquisition? Didn't they want him to get his degree?

They were dancing, now. Heavy feet clumped and stamped up above. These ceilings were like two sheets of hardboard sandwiching a cavity. Why did he have to get thrown out of his digs in town and be moved back into a Hall of Residence?

He knew this album by heart – it was by a band called Loud Shit – and 'Deep Depression' was what passed for a slow, quiet, smoochy number. From here on in, it was pure rending metal, 100 mph on the rpm, accompanied by the sounds of large animals being slaughtered. Most radio stations could not even mention the *title* of the last Loud Shit single they had banned, 'Why Don't You Fuck Off?'. He tried to exclude the din from his thoughts, and summoned all his powers of concentration.

He got a new sheet in the typewriter, and, choosing the keys carefully, at least managed to get his title and name down properly. Then he typed his examination number, and referred to his notes. He had all the quotations, he had the central argument, he even knew exactly what he wanted to say. That put him ahead of most of the others in his seminar group. Except Bloody Basil. That velvet-coated capon must have been born in the Eighteenth Century. No one could have gone through that many obscure philosophical treatises otherwise. He was the kind of slimeball clod who thought epigrams were still in fashion.

The chorus was a couple of decibels louder.

> 'Deep Depressionnnnnn!
> It's the worst by far!
> Deep Depressionnnnnn!
> Makes me feel below par!
> My health is in ruins,.
> And my life is *Hell*!
> Since I caught Deep Depression,
> I don't feel well.'

Pete shut the row out of his head, and launched into his essay. 2,500 words. That was not so much. Five sheets of his typing. And at least 750 words would be eaten up by quotations. Plus a page and a half of bibliography and footnotes. It was almost nothing, really. But, of course, he could not afford to turn in a nothing essay. Pete knew he was on the cusp between a first and an upper second, and this was the one that would tip him either way. This meant the difference between a cushy post-graduate spot researching in the sun in some Californian Summer Camp University and a year of gloomy teacher-training followed by a lifetime of slamming English Lit into the heads of natural born lathe operators in Birmingham. Allowing half an hour to stroll to the Humanities Block, he had six hours. He did not even have to produce a page an hour.

He kept typing, turning scrawled shorthand and under-lined passages from much-used books into something approaching respectable prose. He was getting a headache from trying to type louder than the music.

> 'You meet them in the *café*,
> You see them on the train,
> With the Deep Depression,
> They look like they're in *pain*!
> I read it in the papers,
> I seen it on the news,
> They say Deep Depression
> Is *twice as bad* as the BLUES!'

The pile of books by his bed collapsed, but he was not distracted for more than two seconds. He swivelled in his chair to take in the major volume spill, then turned back to the keyboard. His fingers flew, stubbing on the keys. It was not ten past ten yet, but he was two-thirds of the way down his first page, and gaining . . .

He had books to back him up, but he would not need them. Yesterday, before the essay titles went up, he had been into the library with three extra cards, borrowed from friends. He was a Johnsonian, so he had all the secondary texts out. Taking Bloody Basil's familiarity with Locke and Bishop Berkeley into account, he had grabbed everything hard-to-get on them in the hope of stealing some of the silver-spoon-in-his-mouth slug's thunder. Bloody Basil had his Oxford donship sewn up already. He was practically out of this redbrick hellhole, the bastard. But it was not over yet. Not by a very, very considerable length of calcium carbonate.

The thumping upstairs sounded more like tag-wrestling than dancing. He only knew Thommy slightly, and his orange-haired girlfriend (Clare?) not at all. But he had heard them at nights. When they were not screwing they were fighting. Four o'clock on Friday morning was their favourite arguing time. The York House Student Union Rep called Thommy the RG, which stood for Resident

Git. Clare had bruises sometimes, but it was difficult to tell under her multi-coloured make-up. The mutants were made for each other, Pete thought.

Another chorus of 'Deep Depressionnnnnn!' There was shouting mixed in with the song now, and sound effects from a Sylvester Stallone movie. Grunts and thumps and yelps and cracks. It was as if Thommy and Clare were beating living hell out of each other, then finishing off the job with teeth and claws.

Ten-twenty. First page done. Pete placed it face down on the desk, and had another sheet in the roller before his heart could get to its next beat. He knew his accuracy was way off at this speed, but he could always borrow some Tippex and fix the errors. Once it was on presentable paper, the rest was polishing.

He would have won. It would be all over, three years of study, between drinking, wenching and doping. At least he had been studying all along, not like his best mates Phil, Neil and Stef. They had done two-and-three-quarter years of drinking, wenching and doping, and spent the last term-and-a-bit in panicky over-reading and catching-up. Typical Lower Seconds.

> 'We gotta try to stop it,
> We oughta see it banned!
> There's a Deep Depression,
> Spreadin' through the *land*!
> We need to seek a vaccine,
> We need to find a cure,
> Gotta say, "Deep Depression,
> *Don't Bother Me No More!*"'

Crash!

The whole place shook with that one. Pete bit his tongue, and tasted blood. His little finger got lodged between the 'o' and 'p' keys, and he scraped gouges pulling it free.

Someone screeched over the music. It hardly sounded human. Thommy must have landed a hard one on Clare, put her down for the count. There was banging on the ceiling, and each bang was accompanied by a whiny grunt. Pete knew someone's head was being smashed again and again on the floor of the room above.

He thought he ought to do something, but deep down he knew his essay was more important. He could not afford to play social worker and wind up with missing teeth. Someone must hear all this noise and do something. Soon.

Last chorus, slower and even louder:

> 'Deep Depressionnnnn!
> When will I be free?
> Deep Depressionnnnn!
> Makin' me feel off key!
> My health is in ruins,
> And my life is *Hell*!
> Since I caught DEEP DEPRESSION,
> I DON'T FEEL WELL!'

The words stopped, but the music went on. The banging on the ceiling was in time with the drumbeat now. Pete could hear words – one word – under the bangs.

'Fuck-pig! Fuck-pig! Fuck-pig! Fuck-pig!'

It was a hell of a voice, like the possessed little girl's in *The Exorcist*.

There was nothing for it. Pete knew he had to give up and get involved. No essay was worth more than someone's life. If that was not how he felt, it was how he knew he *ought* to feel. How could he explain to the police that he kept on typing while someone committed murder five feet above his head?

It was easy. *I couldn't hear a thing, officer, I had my Sony Walkman on, loud. Beethoven. Ode to Joy*. It helps me think, gets my ideas in order. I'd miss World War Three that way . . .

'Fuck . . . pig! Fuck . . . pig! Fuck . . . pig!'

No way would PC Plodder believe that. *You're nicked, my son!*

He stopped typing, and listened. The beating went on, and the swearing, and the crying. There was a screeching scratch and a major crash, and the music shut off. The stereo had sustained some severe damage. He stood up, looking around for a weapon . . .

If he was going to separate those two, he would need something pretty hefty to back him up. A bazooka?

In the corner, he saw his tennis racket, unstrung and unused since spring. There are no sportsmen in finals, either. He reached for the racket, but something made him look up.

The gaps between the beats were longer now.

'Fuck . . . . . . pig! Fuck . . . . . . pig! Fuck . . . . . . pig!'

With each blow, the lightbulb jerked like a lynch-mob victim at the moment the noose snaps his neck.

'Fuck . . .'

There were three spots, penny-size, of red on the light brown ceiling.

'. . . Pig!'

Pete cringed, knowing somehow what could come next, knowing what would happen, but horribly unable to do anything about it.

'Fuck . . .'

There was a rending, splintering *crack*! and an abbreviated howl of animal pain.

'. . . Pig!'

The spots were larger now, and more numerous. A droplet gathered on the underside and fell, splashing the back of one of the essay pages. A crack had appeared in the ceiling. The red hissed and smelled on the lightbulb.

'Fuck . . .'

Pete stood like a statue, conscious of the fragility of his flesh. The howling was constant now, louder than the music had been. He could hear other people shouting, thumping on the RG's door, trying to get in on the act.

'. . . *Piiiiiiiiig!*'

A head was forced through the crack in the ceiling, and hung dead above Pete. Most of the skin was gone, and the lower lip had been torn away. One eyeball exploded out of its socket like a crushed *crème* egg. Blood ran in leaky-tap trickles, falling on Pete's hands and face. The thing still shook; whatever was pushing it downwards would not leave off savaging the head's owner.

Pete did not know if it was Thommy or Clare or someone else.

But he did know, as he bent double to regurgitate his breakfast over a scattering of library books, that whoever it was had not got the worst behind them yet.

The head screamed and screamed and screamed. Its owner was still alive.

PART ONE

Out of the Animal Room

Two days before Pete Aston sat down to write about the Age of Reason, Monica Flint, President of the University Students' Union, was feeling silly. With a scarf over her eyes, she was being escorted to a 'secret location' like some John Le Carré character left over from the Cold War. Cazie Bruckner was really pissing her off.

As they drove, nobody talked. Derm played reggae on the Austin's old cassette deck. Monica had no idea where she was going, although she assumed it would be one of those anonymous houses, shared by four or five students, in the sprawl that would have been a suburb if the town planners had got it organized early enough. She guessed Cazie would have Derm drive around at random a bit to make it difficult to judge the distance from the Old Pier, which was where they had picked her up.

Cazie, who had been called Corinne before she came to the University and caught Politics, was functionally insane, Monica thought. No matter what, she would not have been a likeable girl.

Monica had long since given up trying to guess which way the car was going, and was wondering just exactly what it was about Cazie that got up her nostrils. They were both feminists, and agreed on most issues that came up. But one of the things feminism underestimates is women's potential for not getting on with each other.

It could not be jealousy, not really. Cazie came from money – her Daddy was some robber baron industrialist specializing in corporate rape and hostile take-overs – and she did look stunning with her white face and Louise Brooks haircut, not to mention her slim Jamie Lee Curtis

23

thighs. But Monica was not about to underestimate herself; her physical attractiveness was not open to dispute. Since the braces had come off her teeth, she had not had any complaints. There was no *Dynasty*-type catfight between the two women. They did not even have to do business very often.

If only Cazie were not such a self-righteous nut . . .

The car stopped. They were there. The door opened. A hand took Monica by the upper arm and guided her out. She bumped her head slightly on the doorframe. She felt cold night air on her uncovered cheeks.

'Can I take this thing off now?'

A pause.

Monica knew what was happening. Derm and the girl with them, Clare, were looking to Cazie for orders. A nod or a headshake.

It must be the shake.

'Not yet, Mon,' Cazie's Hackney-via-Roedean voice came, 'wait until we're inside. I'm sure you understand.'

'Yeah, quite. Let's get inside before I walk into something, okay?'

'Okay.'

She was helped up a few steps, and reached out to steady herself. She felt curved stone. A pillar. This must be one of those mock-grand porches a lot of terraced hovels in town have. She could not hear or smell the sea, so they must be quite a way from the front. Someone fumbled with keys, and a door opened. Monica could see light through the scarf, and human-shaped figures moving. She was eased over the doorstep and into a hall. The door closed behind her, and, before anyone could give yea or nay, Monica had yanked the blindfold off her eyes.

The light hurt a bit. Spots danced at the edge of her vision.

The hall was entirely conventional. Ragged carpet with a long-lost pattern. Walls in need of massive redecoration

24

and a spot of replastering, covered as best they could be with posters. No pop stars or cult movies, just fliers for demonstrations, glossy pin-ups of endangered species, and stinging indictments of fox-hunting and animal research.

Monica's eyes were caught by a picture of a kitten with an exposed brain, trailing electrodes. That poster did not need a slogan, although it had one, telling you who to blame. Dotted between the big pictures were professional-looking snapshots of red-coated huntsmen brandishing bloody fox portions or white-coated scientists cringing over tortured beagles.

'Through here,' said Cazie.

Monica ducked under a low beam, and felt her way down a flight of narrow stairs into what had been the basement. Now, it was an Operations Room for Cazie's splinter group.

Monica could never remember the acronym. It lacked the elegance and pronounceability of the best factions. There it was, printed in white letters at the top of a cork notice board. STWAA. Stop The War Against Animals.

'Sit down anywhere, Mon.'

Cazie took an armchair in front of the corkboard. Everyone else had to make do with scatter cushions, stools or straight-backed dining chairs. Monica took one of the chairs, and crossed her legs.

'Right, Corinne. Could you please explain this George Smiley stuff?'

The girl looked almost hurt. Someone else had to start for her.

'Monica,' began Derm, the big-shouldered black guy, 'you've got to go easy on the demo tomorrow.'

'*What*!?'

'Hold on, Mon, it's not so simple . . .'

'Corinne, you've spent weeks lobbying the union, packing meetings, getting near to mangling our constitution.

All to get us alerted to UCC presence on campus. You finally manage to prove that animal experiments are being carried out in the Chem Building. And now you want us to backpedal on the protest you've practically organized? What are you people playing at?'

Cazie looked uncomfortable, whiter than usual. Monica began to notice unfamiliar faces at the meeting. Slightly older than she had expected. Not mature students, but outsiders. There was something a little creepy about them, as if they came along with all the spy shenanigans.

'There've been some changes in our strategy, Mon. We've talked to some people, and . . .'

The girl looked around, looked to the new faces for support. All at once, Monica realized Cazie was frightened. It was not a game for girls any more. A cat slid into the room, and weaved its way through everyone before finding its niche in Cazie's lap, nuzzling her denim groin. She stroked it automatically. She really was good with animals.

Finally, someone stepped forward. A man in his late thirties, with a sandblasted outdoors face, wearing a black donkey jacket unmarked by any patches, badges or messages.

'I'm Rex Rote. You've heard of me?'

'Yes,' said Monica. 'You nearly killed a minor member of the Royal Family, right?'

Rote smiled. 'It was war. He wouldn't have got hurt if he hadn't pointed that shotgun at a bird.'

On the first day of the grouse-shooting season, Rote's group had plugged up the gun-barrels of a party of VIPs who were setting out to stride through the heather for a BBC documentary. The filmed explosion had been reasonably spectacular, and still got repeated on news programmes. It had apparently been a highly professional job of sabotage.

'Animals can't fight back for themselves,' said Cazie.

'No,' said Rote, 'so we have to prove that not all human beings are bastards.'

'Fine,' said Monica, 'I assume you're the reason for all this security?'

'I'm still "underground". But I go where I'm needed. And what Ms Bruckner has shown me suggests that I'm needed right here, right now.'

Monica looked at Rote, trying to gauge him. Most of the people she had to deal with on a day-to-day basis were students or faculty. It was not pretend politics, but it was insular, sealed-off from the rest of the world. The gloves rarely had to come off. But Rote probably did not even own a pair of gloves. He was either committed to his cause, or ought to be committed because of it. For a man who spent his life crusading against cruelty, he struck her as a bit of a sadist. He might not hurt a mouse, but he would have no difficulty garrotting a fellow human being.

'Tomorrow,' began Rote, 'you people are going to fuck up everything I've been working for.'

'How?'

'Your piss-little demo, Ms Flint. You'll get a crowd together and shout slogans and maybe get a bit out of hand and break a plate-glass door or two. The local papers will come down . . .'

'Isn't that what you want? The Unwin Chemical Corporation won't like the publicity, and the University certainly won't like being linked to animal experiments. There's a good chance we can force UCC to pull out.'

'Maybe. But a lot of animals will be dead or worse by then. In the short term, all you'll do is make UCC security-conscious. They'll tighten up. Make sure the campus cops spend more time there. They'll know trouble will be brewing.'

'Trouble?'

'Uh-huh. Tomorrow night, there'll be trouble. But

27

better trouble than your placard-waving and slogan-shouting. Effective trouble.'

Monica looked around. Cazie was posed anxiously, her fingers stuck in the cat's fur, seeking approval. Only Rote, and his people, were relaxed.

'What kind of trouble exactly, Mr Rote?'

The man cracked a grin, not a pleasant one, and took a breath.

'Ah well, it's like this . . .'

He had a seminar on the Spanish Civil War to prepare, and Jason was being a pain in the arse.

'Find me a video, Daddy, please.'

The 'please' tailed off into a whine. Brian Connors pushed his chair back from the desk in his study and got up to pay attention to his sometime son.

'Okay, Jase. Give me a moment.'

The eight-year-old vanished from the doorway and was tumbling down the stairs in his inimitable stuntman fashion. Brian followed, realizing for perhaps the tenth time that his body was prepping for the Big Four-Oh next year but one. He had quit cigarettes, but he would never get his young man's lungs back.

With Jean and her new boyfriend in Lanzarote, he could not have refused to take Jason for the week. Even if Jean *had* tried to block his access at the time of the divorce, citing him as an evil and corrupting influence. That was a while back, though. These days, she seemed to be able to stand being in the same room as him without reaching for a breadknife.

Everyone had to mellow, as he knew only too well.

If it were not for Jason, he would have had Debbie around tonight. Then again, though the demands would have been different, the nineteen-year-old was just as capable of distracting him from his work, wearing him

28

down emotionally, leaving his body aching and drained. He had kicked cigarettes into touch, was holding off on the Jamieson's, and had not played his Jimi Hendrix albums in over six months, but he was still sleeping with his students.

It would probably kill him in the end.

Jason was scrabbling through the cabinet in which Brian kept his tapes. His pyjama bottoms hung low on chubby hips.

'What's this, Daddy, what's this?'

Jason held up a tape, label outwards. *Ways of Seeing, Ways of Being*.

'University stuff, Jase.'

The boy was disappointed and distressed. He stuck out his lower lip, and threw the cassette back. Then he had another one out. He made a pretence of examining the spine, then held it out to Brian.

Eight years old, and the kid still could not read. Not even *Janet and John*. Jean said he was just a slow learner, but Brian had already checked out a couple of books on dyslexia, and made a few tentative stabs at getting Mike Prickett, his friend from SocSci, together with the kid. In the pub after their weekly badminton binges, Mike had tried to damp Brian's fears, but there was no getting round it. Jason was a thicko in other ways too. He still could not dress himself properly, as Brian had found out two mornings ago.

Brian looked at the tape. It was one of his under-the-counter jobs, slipped him by an assistant in the Communications Department, *Sixth Form Girls in Chains*. Debbie liked that kind of thing.

'Boring, Jase,' he explained. 'University stuff.'

'Why do you have a boring job, Daddy?'

Sometimes Daddy asks himself that, Jase, he thought. 'It's not boring when you're a grown-up. You'll see.'

'Couldn't you be a fireman?'

Brian laughed and picked his son up.

'Throw me against the roof, Daddy.'

Brian tossed Jason out of his arms, not hard enough to throw him against the ceiling. Jason reached up, and his fingers brushed plaster before gravity pulled him down to his father's grasp.

'On-Cor! On-Cor!'

Brian threw again, the heaviness going out of his chest. Jason could be a lot worse kid really. When his arms got tired, he would dig out the *Teenage Mutant Hero Turtles* episodes he had taped especially, and get back to news coverage of the Spanish Civil War.

The doorbell rang. Debbie?

When they had moved into the campus cottage, Jean had teased Brian about the doorbell. Its double chime was so conventional, so middle-class. With his reputation, he ought to have one that played the North Vietnamese National Anthem. That was when he had known he was finally grown up. Three weeks later, he had shaved his beard, and seen a responsible member of society in the mirror.

The bell rang again, and again. Urgently. It did not feel like Debbie.

He caught Jason, and put him down. In two strides, he was in the hall. A female shape stood behind the frosted glass. He smiled, ready to pull Debbie over the threshold into an embrace. Raphael and Shredder would keep Jason distracted, and the Spanish Civil War could wait . . .

He opened the door, and reached for the girl.

'Brian!'

His hands found a shoulder and a waist, and he pulled. He bent towards her, to kiss . . . and saw red hair.

Debbie was blonde, with occasional purple tints.

'Brian.'

Monica was laughing. She struggled free from him.

'Who were you expecting?'

30

'Uh . . . well . . . hello, Monica, come in. I've just got some coffee going.'

Monica eased past him in the narrow hall. Her body briefly shared airspace with his, and he felt a twinge of arousal. Monica had been after Jean, but before the students. Actually she had been a student, but not like the others. Not like Debbie. Not like *a* Debbie.

She knew her way about the house. In the front room, she collided with Jason. From the doorway, he saw the boy hug her.

'Monneemonneemonneemonnee!'

'Jaysunnjaysunnjaysunn!'

It took a moment for him to realize he was not calling her 'mummy'. He had nearly done so, for a while. Jason had his fingers in her masses of hair, stroking and pulling.

'Ouch. Jason, the wedding's off!'

Suddenly, the child's hands were behind his back. Brian knew his son had a crush – he was not backwards in *everything* – on Monica Flint, and had pestered her to marry him for over six months three years ago. He thought the kid would have grown out of that by now, been embarrassed by it, even. Jason might not have inherited his father's academic bent, but he was well equipped with Brian's other quirks.

As Monica played with Jason, pinching his cheeks and saying how much he had grown, Brian tried to remember the exact words she had used the last time they had met in his house.

He thought aloud, '. . . reprehensible . . . juvenile . . . satyriasis-suffering . . . intellectually-overreaching . . . louse . . .'

She turned towards him, not playing any more.

'You're a bastard, too, for cherishing the hurt, Brian. You just paid me back, we're even. Now, can we start from scratch?'

Well, Debbie *had* been getting on his nerves. That

relationship was reaching its critical mass about now. And Monica was still Something Special.

'It's not that easy, Monica. I'm kind of involved, but I'm sure we could . . .'

For an instant, her face was a Japanese dragon mask of anger.

'Not like *that*, Brian! Not ever again in a million years like *that*! I need help.'

His twinge went away.

He had called her a couple of things too, 'ball-breaking bitch' chief among them. After Jean, that had been the worst of the break-ups, perhaps because both of them had wanted to cling on even after it was obvious nothing would work out. Still, he did not get to meet damsels in distress every day of the week.

'Help? You've got it. Get that coffee from the kitchen while I settle Jason in front of the video, would you?'

Without argument, she was gone. Jason jumped up and down, shouting, 'Cowabunga, cowabunga!'

'Yes, the Turtles, although it'll rot your brain out. You ought to be graduating to *Star Trek* pretty soon.'

He found the tape, and slotted it in the machine. The television winked on, and cartoons filled the screen. He had told Debbie he was thinking of doing a paper on the marketing phenomenon of the *Teenage Mutant Hero Turtles*, but the truth of it was that he liked crap too. There were nearly three hours' worth of episodes on the tape. That would give him time for Monica.

She was coming out of the kitchen with the coffee. After three years, she remembered – black, no sugar.

'Upstairs, in the study.'

'The study?'

'It's where our . . . where the bedroom used to be.'

She smiled and looked at him sideways. He glimpsed her as a nineteen-year-old. Then it was gone, and he realized what was strange about her.

She was frightened.

'Come on up,' she said, going ahead of him. 'I've got to tell you a story . . .'

'Skippy did something interesting last night,' said Carson.

Dr Xavier Anderton walked along the row of cages that lined the wall of the Animal Room, and peered into the mess that had once been a rabbit.

'He redecorated his cage.'

The wire was bent outwards where the animal had hurled itself at the walls of its environment, and several ragged holes had been chewed or punched through. Skippy – all the rabbits were named after television and film animals – should not have been strong enough to do that. Anderton checked the clipboard hung above the cage.

'Batch 125. *Four ccs*?'

'Last of the sample,' explained Carson. 'I thought we should use up whatever was left.'

It was sloppy, but Anderton did not reprimand his assistant. The death was a puzzle, not a tragedy.

Skippy had evidently done his best to do the utmost damage to his cage, and then turned his destructive fury in on himself. He had opened his body from neck to tail, and spilled organs and entrails. Strings of gut hung from jagged wires. The straw was red and sticky. One of Skippy's pink, dead eyes caught Anderton's attention. Rabbits do not have much range of expression, and what they do have comes from whiskers not eyes. But something in the eye spooked the scientist to the soul.

'Should I call UCC?'

'No, not yet. I'll have to know what this means. Cook up another batch of 125. I'll check the other animals.'

This was not quite what Anderton was after, but it was more intriguing than the total lack of response Leo had

33

yielded so far. Lassie, Flipper, Clarence (who *was* slightly cross-eyed), Cheetah and Francis were nibbling lettuce, sleeping or stretching as expected. But Rikki (for Rikki-Tikki-Tavi) was dead and stiff. No violence, no obvious symptoms, just dead.

And Thumper had melted down.

At first, Anderton thought the rabbit was asleep under the straw, but when he reached into the cage to prod it awake, he touched squishy fur. There was a large lump of semi-liquid grease inside, and it oozed out of the mouth, eyes and anus when the rabbit was touched.

This was even more interesting than Skippy.

'Excuse me, Dr Anderton?'

'Yes?'

Anderton returned to the main laboratory. Carson was there, with Finch.

'Did you know the students have a picket line outside?'

'Not again. What's it about? Has Professor Buckingham been doing any more research on racial characteristics?'

Finch looked disturbed. Nervously, she stroked down her seal-short cropped hair.

'No, doctor. It's about us. About the animals.'

Carson chipped in. 'It had to happen. It's a hot issue.'

Anderton chewed his biro, and thought.

'We're secure-locked. This is supposed to be a sealed environment. So, who gives a ferret's fuck about students? Miss Finch, scrub me a workplace and dig up the instruments. We've got some autopsies to do.'

Cazie had to be on the front line. She could not very well be anywhere else after all the work she had put in.

Thommy, dressed as the White Rabbit from *Alice in Wonderland*, pulled out his fob watch and posed for the three local press cameramen. He raised one paw in a clenched fist salute, and chanted, 'UCC Tortures Me! UCC Tortures Me!'

Otherwise, it was a feeble protest. Cazie could not bear the sympathy she was getting from those not in the know. She wanted to tell them it was not her fault, that they were taking it easy, that Rote was on the case. But she knew better than to mention Rote.

When this was over, she hoped to disengage from the Movement. She was getting interested in the homeless. Lots of good people were getting into Poverty Action. Derm, who knew more about poverty than most of her friends, would be particularly keen. And the others would follow. She could form a chapter of Class War. That would certainly get under Daddy's skin.

She was only in this because she liked animals. She had been one of those rich little girls with ponies, and for years she had planned to be a vet when she grew up. And here she was taking Business Studies, and listening to her father talk about getting into the Firm. Daddy was a fatcat all right, but he did not realize what his little girl could do with the power of a medium-sized finance company behind her. He would have the shock of his life, a bigger shock than he had had when he met Derm.

Monica had shown up early, and given a few instructions to her Rentacrowd people. There had been no trouble. Thommy was getting all the attention with his bunny suit. Cazie had had to give a few sentences to the newspapers. She had made do with handing out a prepared statement, detailing all the evidence against UCC and its history of animal experiments. She had lied, and said they had no specific proof that the UCC-financed projects being carried out in the Chem Building involved animals, but that it was the company, not this particular arm of it, they were protesting against.

Rote was lying low back at her place, back at what he

called the 'safe house'. His real work would come tonight, and tomorrow she would change her life.

'Corinne, can I have a word?'

'Uh, oh, hi Mon.'

Monica Flint was the only person, besides Daddy, who still called her Corinne. She did it on purpose.

In the daylight, away from the STWAA Action Room, Monica looked much older, much more confident, much more powerful. Cazie felt uncertain of herself beside the woman.

'Sure, Mon. Things are going nicely here. We can get a tea from the Chem common room.'

'And cross your own picket line?'

Suddenly, Cazie hated Monica. She put her fisted hands into the pockets of the man's pinstripe jacket she wore over her Animal Rights Now T-shirt, and shivered. It was May, but a cold spring was lingering. It looked like rain.

'I forgot. Sorry.'

'Come with me. There's someone who wants to talk to you.'

Monica led her away from Chem, along the paved pathways that criss-crossed the campus village. The trees were shedding blossom like dandruff. The University was out of town, a community unto itself.

Under a tree, a man sat on a bench, wearing a brown leather jacket and black jeans, watching a little boy – wrapped up warm and with a colourful woolly hat on – playing with model spacemen on the grass. The kid was dive-bombing green aliens with a plastic star cruiser. The man was huddled up, hands in his pockets and collar turned up around his face.

Cazie gripped Monica's wrist, hard. She looked into the woman's face.

'You *told*!'

It was like the ultimate betrayal. Cazie could not deal

with it. She began shaking. She could taste the anger in her mouth, feel it trembling in her voice.

'You *told*!'

'It's okay, Corinne.' Monica broke her grip, and then squeezed Cazie's hand. 'You'll see. Rote won't know. Brian knows what we're doing.'

'Brian?'

'Brian Connors. He's in the Humanities Department. You'll like him. Well, maybe that's putting it too strong. Come on, anyway. It'll be all right, honestly.'

Monica pulled her forward, and sat her down on the bench. The man – Brian – smiled and shook her hand. He was good-looking in a crumpled smoothie sort of way.

'Corinne Bruckner . . . Brian Connors.'

'Hi,' said Brian, looking at her in a way she had just begun to appreciate this last year or so. There was no doubt: he found her attractive. 'Corinne?'

'Cazie,' she said. 'What's this about?'

'You know what it's about, Corinne,' said Monica. 'Rote.'

Cazie could not help looking around, to see if there was anyone within earshot. How many people had Monica told?

'Oh God, Rote.'

'You don't need to tell me about Rote,' Brian said.

'You know him?'

'No. I know plenty of people like him, though.'

Monica cut in, 'Brian used to be . . .'

'Never mind that,' he said, with an undertone of irritation. 'Do you understand what you're getting into? Direct action, right?'

'I don't know.'

'Tonight, your group is going to hit the Chem Building.'

Cazie glared at Monica, who did not flinch. She had obviously told this outsider every damn thing.

'Tell me, Cazie.'

Cazie swallowed her spit, and chewed a fingernail. She thought she had beaten the habit.

'Yes. Tonight. We're going to liberate the animals.'

'Uh huh. Liberate? Fair enough. I don't suppose trying to talk you out of it would do any good?'

'Well . . .'

'I thought not. It's not you who has to be convinced any more, is it? It's Rote.'

'Yes. I suppose so, but . . .'

'How out of your control is this situation?'

She did not want to say it.

'Completely?'

She nodded. 'Rote has brought people in with him. He calls them "soldiers". No one likes them, but no one has a choice. He's been in the house for a week now. Someone gave him STWAA as a contact address. He gets what he wants.'

'He's what we used to call "underground", on the run?'

'He still calls it that.'

'You know that harbouring a wanted man is a criminal offence?'

'I suppose so, but . . .'

'You're afraid to turn him in. Don't worry. I would be too. No one is going to blame you for that. We're not dealing with a non-violent debating-society-type animal lover, here.'

'What am I going to do?'

'What are *we* going to do to you, you mean? As far as I can see, nothing. We'll get it over with, and get you out of it. That's all we can do. He'll go away once he's had his raid?'

'I think so.'

'He'd be stupid not to. Strike, then run. That's the system. I don't really care about rabbits either way, but I'd like to be able to think I can see us through this without anyone getting hurt, so I'm going to make it easy for you.'

Brian dug into his pocket and came up with a keyring.

'I got these from Sparks. He's on campus security, but he's a mate of mine and I trust him. This will get you into the Chem Building, and these open the sealed environment – whatever that is – UCC are paying for. Be bloody careful, and don't do any damage. Just go in, get the animals and come out again. Sparks will cover for you.'

'He *knows*?'

'We haven't been adults forever. He probably does more drugs and listens to worse music than you do. As long as his job is protected, he'll do what he can.'

Brian looked again at the little boy, and shouted, 'Jason, leave that alone. You'll get filthy.'

Monica said, 'You've got homes for Flopsy, Mopsy and Whatever?'

'Yes,' Cazie said quietly, shaken by her sudden, apparent reversion to little girlhood. Monica and Brian were like her parents, fed up but helping her out of trouble for form's sake. Just like the time Daddy had talked the headmistress out of expelling her.

Brian put a hand to her face, and brought it around to look at. He had grey eyes, older than the rest of his face.

'You don't know what you're doing, girl, do you? Listen, back in the '70s, probably in the year you were born, I was a student too. I signed petitions and went on marches and stayed up all night painting placards. I was quite well known for it. Red Brian, Commie Connors, that sort of thing. I never had to go underground, but I got pretty close. It was all stupid stuff, I know that now. I knew that then, but I liked the idea of being a hero. I looked a lot like Che Guevara before I had my hair cut. One night, I got up in a Vietcong uniform and led an assault on the American Embassy in Grosvenor Square. There was a whole bunch of us. We had toy guns, and were a bit – well, a lot – drunk or stoned or whatever. It was like playing soldiers. Only the real soldiers at the Embassy didn't know it was a game. I had a girlfriend with me. They shot her.'

'Dead?'

'No. You'd have heard of it. That kid's her son. She's in Lanzarote. But her left knee doesn't work properly, and it never will. We were stupid. You've got to be sensible, you understand?'

'Yes.'

'I wish I could believe you, Cazie.' His gaze pierced her forehead, probing through her guilty secrets. Then, he looked away. 'Jason, stop that or you'll get *such a smack*!'

The boy ran off, spaceships flying in both hands.

'Excuse me, I've got to chase my kid and put him in the hospital. Be smart, be careful.'

He was gone, and she was alone with Monica. She did not particularly like the President, but she had never envied her before.

'Who was that masked man?'

Monica shrugged. 'Just some bum I used to know.'

'Used to know, Mon. You're stupider than I am.'

'Maybe. I doubt it, though. I'll tell you when you're older. If you *get* older.'

It was still cold, very cold.

Normally, Clarence's feelings were limited. Vague senses: claustrophobia, hunger and sexual frustration. Right now there was something in her life more unsettling than these discomforts. In the last few hours, she had started thinking more complicated thoughts than she was used to. And she was hurting.

Right now, Clarence did not feel much like a rabbit at all. It was as if her insides were changing, outgrowing the rest of her body. She bled from her eyes. She chewed her

40

paws to bloody stumps. She shat a stream of painfully hot pellets. She bit the wire.

Nobody came.

She knew what dogs were. A long time ago, as far back as she could remember, she had been penned in a cage within a cage. There were other animals there. She was allowed to spend time with the other rabbits occasionally. She had been able to have sex and eat grass. There were other kinds of animals besides rabbits in the cages. The quietly vicious, needle-sharp, hissing ones were cats. And the noisy, enormously jawed ones were dogs.

Right now, she felt as if there was a dog inside her, gnawing at her insides, trying to get out of her body. Its teeth were tearing inside her guts, pushing out. The dog was going to eat its way out of her, and she would explode.

In her ears, the noises she was making sounded like a dog's growls.

Still nobody came.

Brian and Monica had not seen much of each other after they split up, but since she had become President of the Students' Union, she had been almost completely out of his circle. Once, at a meeting, they had faced each other over a negotiating table. He knew she had been silently hurt that he had sided with Vice-Chancellor Jackson against the students petitioning for a more open assessments system, and he had felt mildly guilty, remembering the days when he would have been on her side, arguing a good deal more heatedly and violently than she did, and to much less effect. She had been a sharp student, and now, as a post-graduate with a year's sabbatical to discharge her duties as head of the Union, she was an even sharper politician. And she still had that hair.

After talking to Cazie Bruckner, they had had lunch

together – with Jason – in the Refectory, and talked inconsequentially. Without probing, he had found out that she was not emotionally involved. With probing, she had got a good idea of the succession of Debbies who had traipsed through his bedroom in the last few years. She told him he was starting to show his age, and he was not even hurt.

'. . . and you're wearing a tie.'

'A present from Jean. Last Christmas.'

'It doesn't look so bad.'

'I think so.'

They did not talk for a while, and Jason filled in the gap in the conversation with a long story about his schoolfriends' slug-eating activities. Brian lost the thread, and got interested in Monica. She had slight smile lines around her mouth. He mentally calculated her age – twenty-three, twenty-four? Once, he had thought of lining her up as Wife Number Two, but she had not wanted to go along with it. That proved, he supposed, what a smart girl she was.

She was the only student he had ever slept with whose grades he had had to mark down to prevent him being accused of favouritism. Debbie, for instance, might have a great tongue but was stuck with a typical third-rate mind and would be lucky to scrape a C Minus this term.

'Jason's going to a party this afternoon,' he said. 'I've got to drop him off. Want to come by?'

Her lower lip was slightly moist, which he found intensely arousing. She recognized the line, recognized the opportunity for an afternoon with him.

'And Debbie?'

'Who?'

She laughed once, cynically, and shook her head. 'Brian, you don't give up.'

'It's one of my better qualities.'

'Whoever told you that?'

'No one.'

'I'm not surprised. Jason has more shame than you.'

'Wha'?' Jason frowned, not understanding.

'It's nothing, Jase. Auntie Monica was being silly. I hope *you* don't eat slugs.'

'No, they taste horrible.'

'How do you know?'

'Uh . . . I refuse to answer that question on the grounds that I might 'criminate myself . . .'

'What?' spat Monica, laughing.

'Television,' said Brian. 'Jean lets him watch all day. He's fluent in cliché. A year ago, he got obsessed with *Neighbours* and started talking in a 'strine accent all the time. Thank God that's over.'

'Can we go to the party now, Daddy?'

'Sure. Monica?'

'I have to be in my office. There's a UGM at four, and I've got to explain myself on a couple of points.'

'Some other time?'

'Maybe.'

Brian stood up to go, helping Jason on with his hat and scarf. Monica reached out and stroked the boy's cheek, then put her hand on his arm.

'Brian,' she said, 'I want to thank you for today. You've helped a lot.'

'All part of the service, ma'am. I'll just slip back into my Clark Kent disguise and leave without making a fuss. Take care.'

'Yeah. You too.'

At home that afternoon, while Jason was splashing in an indoor paddling pool at his party, Brian started thinking seriously about Monica, remembering. He could not tell one Debbie from another in his mind now, but every detail of Monica was sharp. Her long, warm kisses; her gentle, expert fingering; that strange goulash recipe; her clear, perfect singing voice, unexpectedly coming out when she was distracted.

He phoned Debbie's flat, but hung up before the third ring. He did not know how he felt about anything.

The Campus Radio Collective meeting had been going on for too long, and Eddie Zero was beginning to feel an ache in his drainpipe-jeaned knees from leaning slumped against the wall because all the chairs in the tiny office were occupied by people with seniority. This was not doing his red velvet teddy-boy jacket any good, and he did not think anything else was going to come out of it either. He examined the shine on the toes of his winkle-pickers.

Posie Columba, chairperson of the collective, was announcing the new schedule for the station. She had not got to Eddie Zero's Rock 'n' Roll Rebellion Show yet. Just now, she was outlining her plans to devote every weekday for the next month to a World Music Festival she had been organizing with her friends Achmet and Zorrino. Achmet thought Lloyd Price was a building society, and Zorrino could not tell The Ventures from The Chordettes.

'This is the sort of cutting edge thing CR should be promoting,' Posie said, her *okay-yah* voice sandpapering Eddie's ears. 'It's authentic, yah, and it's the wave of the future.'

She actually had said 'yah' and expected people not to laugh at her. No one had laughed at her, and he managed to pass off his own snort as a cough. She looked at him with too-narrow eyes, and went on with her spiel.

Eddie stifled a yawn, and amused himself by imagining he was the masked mangler, star of a slice 'n' dice movie in which a collective of campus radio jocks are killed off

44

one by one in ways appropriate to their programmes. Funkmaster Dee, the worst-dressed white boy Eddie had ever seen, would be plugged into a sound system and booted to death by the throb of his own dance albums. Psychedelic Pstan, who never played a track less than three-quarters of an hour long, would be juiced up on hallucinogenics and dipped, in his squiggle shorts and big red glasses, into a vat of steaming chemicals at the world's first Acid Bath Party. Shaggy Andy, who was a folk traditionalist, would be flayed alive by country craftsmen who took a pride in their work and stretched his skin over the bole of their mandolins to get a better sound. And Posie would be forced to drink a gallon of water from each of the Third World countries she reckoned were musically in the forefront of civilization, and then be rotted from the inside by 57 different varieties of horrible disease. He would let Achmet and Zorrino off only if they agreed to clean up the mess.

They had argued about music all year, and Eddie was fed up with it. All he wanted to do was unleash some real rock 'n' roll onto the airwaves, and let the kids out there develop an appreciation of genuine musical genius. His pantheon was Buddy, Elvis, Jerry Lee, Chuck, Ritchie, Little Richard. Everything else sucked. Posie said he was 'a throwback to the pop mentality' and called him an imperialist racist for writing off African and South American music as 'ear-jerking crap'. What kind of colour was Harvey Fuqua, bitch?

'Every day of the week, we'll spotlight a different country, right?' Posie said, cheeks red and shaking with teary enthusiasm. 'Monday, Zimbabwe. Tuesday, Brazil. Wednesday, Gabon . . .'

'Posie, when are you going to fit in Antarctica?' he asked.

The girl frowned again, and made a tent with her porky fingers.

'What kind of music do they got in Antarctica?' said Funkmaster Dee, trying to sound as much like a fifty-year-old black pimp from Detroit as is possible for the teenage Caucasian son of a Coventry vicar.

'If you can't be serious, we'll have to propose a motion to censure you, Eddie.'

'Oh, please, Hot Mama, don't censure me. Anything but that.'

Posie smiled a mean, devious smile, and told them all when their slots were.

Eddie's show was between two and three A.M. on Fridays.

Rote had shown them how to black up like the SAS. Clare felt strange in her balaclava and heavy coat. She was used to colours.

She and Thommy sat in the back, with Cazie and Rote's three soldiers. Rote was up front, with Derm. Derm was driving. It was an anonymous van, dark green and unmarked. Rote had made sure it was parked around the campus for a few days, to get the security people used to the sight of it. Rote had turned up at Cazie's in it, and Clare wondered if it might be stolen.

Thommy had got some speed to take earlier, but Rote had seen him give her some and forbidden them. He had slapped Thommy with his open hand and told him not to act like a prat.

Clare was afraid of Rote, but agreed with him about Thommy. This was no time to be out of your head. She could not help but feel good, seeing the glint in Thommy's eyes as Rote hit him, the glint that meant he was too chicken to hit back. Thommy was free with his hands usually – he must have been a bully at school – but Rote was in a different class altogether.

Last night, after the meeting, Rote had taken her

upstairs and they had fucked. Thommy had not been happy about that either. Clare was not sure how happy she was about it, in fact, but she had had to go along with it. Once in the sack, she had been able to give up thinking and just get into the fucking. This morning, she had bruises, blue weals up and down her thighs and angry red dots around her nipples. No wonder Rote was so concerned with the protection of animals; he was one.

They drove out of town, towards the campus. There was a double carriageway, but it was practically empty. Clare felt fear and excitement in the pit of her stomach. Her breasts hurt.

With a trace of self-disgust, she realized that she was almost turned on. She squirmed a little on the hard bench, as if her arse were itching. Thommy was oddly withdrawn, sober. Clare's mouth went dry, as she realized she did not know which she would be fucking tonight. Thommy or Rote.

For once, Cazie was quiet. She looked strange with her face streaked commando-style, and a black beret pulled over her ears. There were snailtracks of white on her cheeks. Clare realized the girl was crying.

The soldiers were like robots. Two men and a woman, switched off when not in use. They came with Rote. It was funny. They did not even talk about animal rights or press campaigns like the rest of STWAA. They were only interested in doing damage, in hurting people. In a week, they had not even told anyone their names. Security, she supposed.

The van stopped.

'We're here,' said Rote, from up front. 'Get ready.'

Clare tensed, aware that she would need to go to the loo in the very near future. She ran over the plan in her mind, as Rote started putting it into action.

Rote got out of the van. One of his men made sure the back door was unlatched. Rote walked up to the double doors of the Chem Building, keys in hand. His soldiers had jemmies and boltcutters in case the keys were a bust. But they did their job properly.

'Now,' Derm said.

They all piled out of the van in an orderly fashion. Clare pushed against Cazie, and could feel the girl shaking. Rote's woman shoved them both, and they went with the team. Rote had the door open, and counted them all inside. Derm stayed at the wheel of the van, lying quiet on the front seat. It was properly parked. No one should get curious.

Inside the building, Thommy and Clare got out their torches and, in silence, made their way down the corridor towards the sealed environment. The further they got from the glass doors, the better Clare felt. Once they were swallowed by the complications of the building, there was no chance they would be seen. It was dark, but familiar. The place was just like every other building on campus, a beehive of lecture halls, offices, store-rooms and laboratories.

Rote had done his homework. They made no false turns. UCC had obligingly put up a notice detailing their contributions to the University, marking out the laboratory where they were carrying out their research. Clare knew rabbits were being tormented in the facility, but it struck her now that she had never heard exactly what they were suffering for.

Rote opened the first sealed door, and then the second. The air did not feel any different inside the laboratory, although it was supposed to be purer. Clare was studying History; she did not know anything about the procedures here.

'Where are the animals?' said Thommy, his voice squeaking a little, like Mickey Mouse.

'There.'

48

Rote took Thommy's wrist, and pointed his torch at a sign.

ANIMAL ROOM.

The door was wooden, inset with a wired glass window. It was locked. Cazie's source had not furnished a key for this one.

'Smash it,' said Rote. His male soldiers stepped forward. One tested the handle, tapped the wood around the lock, and nodded to the other. The second man aimed a lightning-fast martial arts kick at the indicated spot. The door shot inwards, and slammed against something. Orange wood showed through white paint where the door had splintered.

There was a chattering and growling inside the Animal Room.

'Get the cages, and let's get out.'

Something shot out of the Animal Room, and struck Clare full in the chest. It was harder than any of the blows Thommy had ever landed on her. She fell backwards onto a fixed table, slamming her lower back against a hard edge.

The thing was still on her, clinging to her shirt. She felt points of pain on her breasts. Her torch was gone, and she could not see the thing. It could not be a rabbit. Rabbits do not have claws. It was making noises like a horror movie monster. She grabbed the furry creature, and pulled it away. Her shirt – and her skin – tore. The thing had fishhooks in its feet.

Clare felt the dampness spreading in her jeans. She thought she might have snapped her spine, but she could still kick and fight so she must be all right. Her back hurt like a bitch though.

'Shit!'

Rote had Thommy's torch now. Clare was rolling on the floor. He directed the beam at the thing she was holding up. It *was* a rabbit, but not like any rabbit she had ever seen before.

Its teeth shone red, and then it twisted in her grasp and kicked free.

'Don't move,' Rote said. 'Something is loose.'

Cazie helped her up, and put her arms around her. They were both crying out loud now.

'Shut up!' It was the other woman, Rote's soldier. She had Clare's torch.

Rote threw light into the Animal Room. There was a row of exploded cages. Straw was on the floor, and things were moving incredibly fast under the light. They came out of the room and spread out into the lab, hiding under tables, benches, sinks. They were furred, but fast as mercury on an incline.

'The animals are out. That's what we wanted. Let's move! We go now!'

'Rote,' shouted Cazie, forgetting all need for quiet, 'we've got to collect them. They'll just be recaptured. We've fixed up homes . . .'

Rote shone his torch full at Clare, dazzling her. She knew how she must look.

'Take a gander at that, Bruckner! If you want to pet something with a disposition towards that kind of rough stuff, it's up to you. The rest of us are pulling out!'

'He's right,' said Thommy. 'Move it.'

Rote led them as if it were a retreat. Clare could not move, but when the torches were out of the lab she could hear the things moving around her. Something ran over her feet. She ran through the sealing doors and caught up with the torchlight. They followed her.

'Help,' she whispered.

Only Cazie turned. A furball collided with a wall, bounced, and ran up the girl's leg. Clare could not do anything. Cazie grunted sharply as teeth rent through her sweater. A tear opened white down her arm, and then a

50

line of blood appeared. She slammed her arm, and the thing on it, against the wall. The rabbit screeched and burst.

There was a mess, and Cazie was spattered from head to foot. The girl could not stop screaming. Red and purple lumps dripped from her face and chest, and she frantically wiped at herself, trying to get the blobby filth off her.

It took Thommy and one of the soldiers to get Cazie moving again. They left the exploded animal on the wall, and went towards the main door.

There was someone between them and the outside. Derm? No, someone in a peaked cap. Someone with a uniform.

Rote reached out his hand behind like a surgeon requesting an instrument, and one of the soldiers gave him a jemmy.

'Stop,' said the shadow. 'Security.'

Rote swung the jemmy like a baseball bat, and connected with the figure's head. The cap went flying, and the man was down. Rote paused to deliver two more professional blows. The guard did not make a sound after the first *oof*. Clare knew something must have broken inside him. She thought she had heard a punching crack that might have been his skull fracturing.

'Leave him for the rabbits,' said Rote, holding the door open.

Derm was outside. He did not ask any questions, just got the van started. In the back, in the darkness, Clare started to feel her own hurts. Waves of pain shot through her body. Cazie was having unattended hysterics, babbling incoherently, and lashing out in the darkness at anyone who came near.

Orange light passed through the van at intervals as Derm drove under the streetlamps. In these flashes, Clare

51

saw Rote's scary, feral grin. Then she curled up, and blacked out.

It was six-thirty in the morning, and Brian was naked in his bed – thankfully alone – when Jason came into his room as if it were Christmas morning, and jumped up and down on him.

'Uhhh, Jase, what is it?'

'Daddy, Daddy . . .'

He looked at his bedside digital clock and did not believe it. Without his contacts in, the world looked fuzzy and unfinished.

He repressed the urge to become the father of an abused child, and smiled sweetly at his son.

'Couldn't it wait, Jase?'

'Daddy, Daddy . . .'

It was light out, a grey light that could just be working up to the first sunny day of summer. But right now, it was cold enough to goose-pimple him all over under his thin duvet.

Brian sat up, feeling an ache in the pit of his stomach where Jason had landed too hard on him. He got hold of his son and stopped him moving. Even if he was unable to calm the kid down, he should be able to prevent him doing injury to himself and others.

'I've found a rabbit, Daddy,' said Jason, eyes alight. 'Can we keep it?'

As usual, Frank Lynch had slept for barely two hours. He was generally getting restless. It had been too long.

He had read until five o'clock, about Napoleon in Egypt, ignoring the woman in bed next to him. Theresa never noticed when he was not sleeping. It was not one of their sex nights. Finally, he had to join her for his few hours – dreamless, almost catatonic. When he woke up, she was gone.

He could not remember her speaking to him during the last few days. That had to be an illusion. They were just in one of their routine ruts. It sometimes happened, between assignments.

He was washed, shaved, showered and finished before Darren and Tracy were up. In any case, the children – well, junior adults – would not have interrupted his routine. He had had his own bathroom put in, adjoining the mini-gymnasium he had designed and built himself.

Looking after his body was important, a part of his job, and he should not have to share his space with anyone else while he was about it. He had caught Darren using his shower once, and given him a demonstration of his need for privacy. He was skilled enough not to leave a mark on his son, but the boy would remember the pain long after he had forgotten his excuse.

Lynch did not think of himself as a brutal man; but he knew the value of direct action. Darren would never again set foot in his father's space. A lesson had been driven in.

For an hour, Lynch did push-ups, pull-ups, sit-ups. Then he punched and kicked the bag. He was as fast as ever, but still worried about his heart rate. He could control his breathing, knew how much to drink to stop himself over-heating, and could work out any aches in his limbs, but there was no way he could do anything to slow down wear and tear on that big muscle nestled in the cage behind his slablike pectorals.

Theresa had his table ready when he was finished. Milk, orange juice, high-fibre cereal, and a well-done steak with green salad. No sweets, no sugar, no coffee. She had even laid out the *Telegraph* for him. Darren and Tracy were spooning down dollops of wheaty pulp and yoghurt, without much enthusiasm.

Occasionally, Lynch reflected with satisfaction that he would probably outlive his children.

There was no talking at the table. It was a week-day; Tracy was going to school, Darren to college. Neither had been out last night. He had not checked to see if they had done their homework, but he felt confident that they had. The first time he had caught Tracy skipping homework, he had snapped twenty-five of her records, one after another. It was not supposed to be easy to break vinyl.

He was set up for a day much like yesterday and tomorrow. Exercise, diet, reading, thinking. He had been on this course too long, resting, waiting. He had to be ready at the slightest warning, but knew you could over-train, stretch your nerves too far, and fall apart through *lack* of stress.

After the children were gone, he completed the *Telegraph* crossword in seven minutes fifteen seconds – two minutes and thirty-eight seconds over his record – and read the front page. Strikes, elections, terrorism, lawsuits, and the Royal Family. Josh Unwin, described as a 'Chemical Baron', was meeting the Prime Minister to give economic advice, following his suggestion that the country would be a better place if it were run like his corporation. A missing pro-Paisley councillor in Northern Ireland had turned up in a roadside ditch with a bit from a Black and Decker drill embedded in his brain.

Then he got dressed, in slimline body armour and regulation jumpsuit, and went into the cellar room to look after his guns. The room was double-locked, and banned to everyone else, although he had to let Theresa in twice a week to vacuum. Dust and dirt were the first enemies of any good soldier.

His pictures were on display in the workroom. There were not many of them – obviously, his efficiency in the business would be compromised if he had to stop and pose for snapshots every few minutes – but he was pleased with the few he did have, as much for the way you had to look twice to see him in them as for the record of his achievements. There he was at Goose Green, blending in with the paras, and there in Ulster, outside the ruin that had once been an IRA bomb factory. They were from the time before he joined the UCC CSD.

Then there were the other pictures, grainy and clipped from front pages or photocopied from files. They showed just faces, mainly, some posed and grinning, some mashed and broken. Palestinians, Iranians, Iraqis, Argies, Micks, nationless vermin, slit-eyed fanatics, a few simple security risks, inconvenient bystanders. All his.

He took an Uzi out of the rack, and began to strip it down. Just as he was reaching for the baby oil, he heard his telephone klaxon sound.

He was on call. The waiting was finished. All over the city, beepers would be sounding, and his men would be scrambling.

He picked up the receiver. He did not have to say anything. The familiar, but nameless, voice gave him the facts like a newsreader delivering a prepared statement.

He felt alive again.

Jason was crying. His rabbit had died before Brian could even get up and take a look at it.

There was something funny about this dead thing. It was unmistakably a rabbit. It had probably been run over by a car. It certainly had been squashed in some way, and Brian thought he felt broken bones inside the corpse. But there was something more wrong about it than the mere fact of its deadness. It was as if it had died angry, with its claws out.

'Where did you get him, Jase?' he asked, trying to reach through his son's grief, hoping to distract him with the mystery.

'Came . . . through . . . window.'

'Oh yes. Show me.'

Jason took his father's hand, and led him into the spare room where he was sleeping – the room that had been his when he and his mother shared the house on campus with Brian. His bed was a mess, and the window was open. There were reddish-brown smears on the windowpane and the sill. Brian saw three hard, black pellets on top of the dressing table, and more blood where Jason said he had found the rabbit.

'It was alive.'

'I'm sure.'

'It's not a very pretty rabbit, Daddy.'

'No.' It certainly was not. Especially not now, and probably not when it had been bouncing around.

'It doesn't have white gloves like Bugs Bunny.'

'Not many rabbits do.'

The front of Jason's pyjama jacket was a bloody ruin. It was a good thing his mother was on an island thousands of miles away.

'It wasn't a very happy rabbit, Jason. I think it's probably better off dead.'

'And in Heaven?'

'If you like.'

Heaven? Where did he get that? From school, probably. Jean was as agnostic as he was. Or had been. Who knows? People change.

'Only . . .'

'Yes.'

'Only . . . at the end . . . when it was dying . . . it was bad . . . mightn't God notice?'

'It doesn't count. You aren't yourself when you're dying.'

He looked out of the window. The sun had come up. It would be a nice day. Should he try to get in touch with Monica? There might still be something there.

If there was not, there was always Debbie. The trouble there was that having Debbie over meant going through her last essay, a generous D+, before anything else.

The playback in his head stuck on something Jason had just said: 'it was bad . . .' What did that mean?

'Jason, how was the rabbit bad?'

'Oh, it doesn't hurt any more.'

'What?'

'The bite. See.'

His son rolled up a sleeve to reveal a white, plump little arm. Jason had not bled much, but the tooth-shaped cuts were still visible.

PART TWO

The Freak-Outs

Security was out in force. Monica had to drive through two checkpoints to get on campus. The place was getting like South America. None of the polite uniforms could or would tell her what was up, but she had this horrible feeling . . .

She parked in her usual space by the Union Building, and went up the backstairs to her suite of offices off Mandela Hall. No one else was in yet. The front desk should at least be manned . . . oops, personnel. A pile of mail had been dumped in the old milk crate by her door, mostly tubed magazines.

She sat at her desk, and leaned back in her swivel chair. Her back was starting to ache already. She ought to change her mattress, she knew. She was still worked up from yesterday – from Cazie, from Brian, and from the disastrous UGM.

She knew that she had come close to being the Richard M. Nixon of student politics yesterday. If the Broad Left Alliance and the Left Caucus had been able to agree on a wording for the motion, the student body would have impeached her. It was not her fault, it was not anyone's fault, but she was a Libertarian Socialist and they were out of favour in the Movement at the moment, for flirting with notions of a free market economy. It was just a bloody label.

There was too much to worry about – Union Societies haggling for a slice of the funding, the University Authorities trying to get their programme of spending cuts implemented, the threat of decreased quotas for overseas students, everyone from the miners to the Sandinistas

61

begging for the students to be in solidarity with them and shell out for the privilege. Plus the eternal niggling doubt that this had nothing at all to do with the day-to-day life of her average student constituent. At the last election, the Apathy Society candidates had polled surprisingly well.

She had heard too many times that she had been elected because of her nice smile, blue eyes and red hair. Sometimes she was attracted by the prospect of resigning and getting back to her post-graduate research. There was even a real world out there somewhere beyond the three small hills that bounded the campus community, bunching it up close to the main road. She had spent her whole life being educated; it was time she did something else.

Then Lindy Styles, her Vice-President/Communications, came in, along with Berenice, the secretary.

'There are campus cops all over the place,' said Lindy, 'and real police. Something's up in Chem.'

'Oh shit. Any ideas?'

'No, but it's heavy. They've put up yellow Do Not Cross tapes and are guarding them. Perhaps the demo yesterday put the wind up UCC?'

'Some fucking hope, Lindy. Bern, could you call the switchboard and see if anyone knows anything? I've got a bad feeling.'

The secretary took off her coat and bag, and started pushing buttons on the phone. After a while, she got through to someone, and talked for a few moments. She rung off.

'Someone's been hurt . . . a guard, last night.'

'What? Badly?'

'Tisa didn't know, but it seems so.'

'Shit shit shit.'

'The police were here early. There's been a break-in as well.'

'Those fucking idiots.'

'Pardon?'

'Just idiots in general, Bern. How about some tea? I think it's going to be a nasty day.'

'It looks quite nice outside.'

'I mean inside, Bern.'

'Oh, right.'

The secretary vanished into her tea-making alcove, and Monica heard the tap going. 'Lindy,' she said, 'I'm going to have to take care of this, I think. If anyone comes over or calls to hassle me, could you put up with it, please?'

'Sure.'

'I love you.'

'I know that. I love you too.'

'That's just hunky-dory, then, eh?'

Alone in her own office, Monica dug out her address book. She did not have a number for Cazie Bruckner, and a call to University Records could not get her one either. Because of all that pissing about, she did not even know where the girl lived. She considered calling the hospitals and the police station, but decided to put that off until she had a better idea of what had gone on last night.

After a long pause for thought, she dialled Brian's number from three-year-old memory.

Cazie had gone to bed feeling like shit warmed over, and cried herself to sleep. Now, waking up, she felt terrific.

She was instantly alert, not at all bleary. All her aches and pains were gone. Sitting up in bed, she tingled as the sheet fell, the cotton brushing her nipples. She held out her arm, her torn arm, and could only see a fine pink thread where she had been cut. She was better.

And she was hungry.

She got up and slipped her robe on. Her movements felt strange, catlike. She sensed a strength, a suppleness in her limbs, she was unused to. It was as if she had done a year's worth of aerobics in her sleep.

Last night?

She remembered. She had been overwrought, and had practically fallen apart during the trip home. She had been hurt, although that now seemed like something that had happened to her when she was a very little girl, and so had Clare. Thommy had split with Clare, and taken her to his room in York House. Derm had driven the rest of them back. He would be sleeping on the couch downstairs, now.

Suddenly, she wanted Derm.

They had been lovers for two months, but she had never needed the boy as crucially as she did now. Needed him to pound his big black cock into her slim pink slit.

At the back of her mind, she was shocked. She did not think like that, usually. There was more than just sex with Derm. Despite his muscle-man physique, he could be surprisingly sensitive, and there was a ball of dispossessed social anger inside him that excited her. Sometimes, she had thought it was mainly the need to upset Daddy. He felt threatened by black people, and she knew he could not stand the thought of her with Derm. That had been one of the most attractive things about the boy. But this morning it was just sex.

If only Rote and his soldiers were not in the front room too, laid out like corpses in their combat camouflage sleeping bags. She yawned, feeling the cool air on the back of her throat, and stretched her entire body. Up on her toes. Legs, back and arms taut. Fingers out like claws. She rolled her head, and felt spasms of muscular pleasure in her neck, and all down her spine.

She touched her breast, lightly teasing the nipple with her thumb and forefinger. Uncontrollably, she came. It was like electro-convulsive therapy. She fell into a crouch, amazing tingles coursing through her thighs. It was like some twisted form of sexual epilepsy. She sucked down gulps of air, and clutched at the carpet. Shutting her eyes tight, concentrating on her body, she regained control and was all right in herself again.

Looking at the carpet, she saw the five slashes where her nails had torn.

He had just finished giving instructions to Abigail, the student he was entrusting Jason to for the day, when the telephone rang.

'Hello, Brian, it's . . .'

'Monica, good to hear your voice.'

'Yeah, it's . . .'

'Hold on a minute, would you.'

He turned to Abigail, a fragile girl who looked about fourteen but was reputed to be a potential First, and pointed at his son, who was already scratching at the bandage around his arm. Abigail caught him, and gently pulled his fingers away. He looked to be stronger than her, but she used persuasion. She took Jason into the next room, leaving Brian to his call.

'Sorry about that. Jase's got a war wound, and he keeps making it worse.'

'Oh, I hope it's not . . .'

'. . . not serious. Don't worry. Bitten by a rabbit. Not even a hint of rabies around.'

'Great. I'm afraid I've got bad news. Cazie . . .'

'Shit. How many dead?'

'That may not be a joke, Brian. I haven't got the story straight yet, but a guard was hurt. I don't know how much anyone else knows, but there are policemen all over the place. What have you got on today?'

'Nothing. Uh, well, invigilating, but I took Rob Bickford's place on Tuesday so he could be on the radio. He'll step in for me. Do you want me to start digging into the case? I was always a big Philip Marlowe reader.'

Monica was quiet at the end of her line.

'Like I said, Brian, this may not be funny any more.'

'Sure, sure, sure. I'm not going to be in the combat zone, you know. I'll just drop by Sparks's place for a chat. He'll be going spare anyway if the key stunt backfired. Then I'll be around the Union Building, say, for lunch. We could make a habit of it.'

'Jason?'

'Taken care of. I'm not being shown up by my own son. Not yet, at any rate.'

'See you later then.'

'Later.'

Click.

Brian finished his long-neglected cup of coffee. At least, he took two swallows of the cold stuff, gargled and spat it out in the sink. Out of the kitchen window, he could see Abigail and Jason.

The kid would wear her out. He was throwing frisbee, and Brian only now realized how good Jason had got. A few weekends back, he had had to struggle to catch one in ten throws, now he was not missing at all. And Abigail was having to run as if she were one-on-one with Billie Jean King in her prime. He could not help noticing the girl's calves as her peasant skirt lifted when she ran. Despite the ankle socks and trainers, she did not look as young as he had thought.

At least Jason was ignoring his wound now. He seemed to be positively bursting with energy.

Derm was out of his depth.

As he sat on the bog in Cazie's place, straining over the daily bowel movement his mother had prescribed as the key to eternal youth and vigour, he wondered how the hell he had become mixed up with midnight raids and brained security guards, not to mention whale-loving terrorists and power-crazed rich kids.

As usual, he supposed, he was just trying to get laid.

He had been into sports at school because it was as good a way as any to get into Marie-Jeanette Traherne's navy blue knickers. And he was too good to lie low. Unlike most Incredible Hulks, he could run a mile in six minutes without perspiring hard. And he could stand stock still in front of a speeding locomotive. Well, maybe a speeding go-cart. In the States, he would have been a natural for American Football. Here, it was soccer or nothing. Until he had got into rugby.

Not many Brixton black kids make it in rugby. Derm did not know why. It was his game, and he was the best his school could come up with. Now, while he was peripherally studying Human Biology, he was the star of the *real* all-black rugby team, the Bantu Warriors. His ambition was to violate the Gleneagles Agreement by going onto a field with fifteen double-dyed Afrikaaner white racists and putting them all out of the game forever. Sometimes, he dreamed about it. He felt the slams, heard the bones breaking, tasted the blood.

Now, Crazy Cazie had got him into a position where he could, quite conceivably, go to jail. Her thighs were fine wine, but no pussy was worth that much.

White women! Jesus H. Christ! Why couldn't he do like that song from *West Side Story*, 'Stick To Your *Own* Kind'?

After all the dramatics last night, he had hoped to get something back for it. Some people are really turned on by breaking the law. He had never really got through to Cazie in bed, and he was proud enough to be bothered by it. Last night should have seen some good loving in her single bed, but she had got herself chewed open by some kind of mutant bunny and he had had to crash out on the sofa. In the same room as Rote's Death Squad. Shit in a shopfront, what was happening?

He finished his job, and did the paperwork. The ancient plumbing took forever to finish, and sounded like an earthquake when it did.

Cazie was waiting for him outside the loo.

'Sorry to keep you waiting, Caz. You okay?'

The girl looked at him weirdly, and Derm remembered all his Jamaican Grandmammy's scare stories about haints and *zombis* and shapeshifters. Cazie had changed somehow.

'I'm better.'

'That's good. Let's get some fried bread and bacon going.'

'No, not yet. Come into my room, quickly.'

She darted away, behind her door. She had touched him, trailing her fingertips from his neck downwards, across his chest – he could feel the points through his thick dressing gown – as far as his hip. It was as if an acupuncture needle had hit the spot precisely. He had an instant hard-on that parted his dressing gown.

In her room, she was naked. Not naked as she had been the other times, under the covers, with the lights out. Properly, brazenly naked. Her shoulders were rotating slightly, as if she were dancing to unheard jazz. Her legs were spread, and Derm could see the muscles clenching under the smooth skin of her thighs.

'Come here.' It was an order, and yet a desperate plea. She did not need to say it twice.

He tugged at the knot of his dressing gown, and it fell. The cord brushed his jutting penis, and he felt as if he would come immediately, before he had even touched her.

Her hands came for his shoulders, and pulled him down on her. He slid home smoothly as she stifled a scream.

68

Her vulva gulped, and he was swallowed, held fast, almost painfully.

'Fuck me, nigger. Fuck me now.'

This was not Cazie, the lily-skinned liberal who would rather be boiled in oil than espouse an unfashionable cause, the girl who traded her body for street credibility. This was some other fantastic tart dressed in her silky skin.

But Derm was past caring.

They moved together, astonishingly fast. He was sure she had peaked early, but she was not put off her stroke. He came, and lost his breath and his rhythm, but she kept bucking under him, forcing him to follow her lead. She sucked air beside his ear, then bit him, hard. He might have been bleeding. Her neck arched up, and she fastened a kiss over his mouth before he could protest.

When he finished spurting inside her, the knob of his penis ached. His erection was dwindling. But faster and faster she moved, and more desperately she sucked at his mouth, trying to draw all the air out of him. Her tongue was in his throat like a snake, stifling him.

He broke free, and tried to protest, but she rolled and – with a strength he would never have expected from her – flipped him onto his back. She rode him high, coaxing him hard again with vaginal spasms and rough fingernail traces just above his pubic hair.

He tilted his head back over the edge of the bed and looked at the ceiling. She was howling, in what must be a continuous orgasm. He climaxed again, then lost it. He might as well be dead, but she kept working on him.

She moved back and forth, her knees raked his sides, and her nails began to dig in. There was definitely blood now. Her hands came to his face, the first three fingers of each extended like an inexpert typist's. She stroked his cheeks with razorblade tenderness.

He could taste the blood, inside his mouth. She had

gone deep, perhaps all the way to his teeth. He was too exhausted to yell.

'Tribal scars, nigger,' she screeched, 'tribal scars!'

The pain began, and he knew he had to fight her off or die.

He feebly tried to push her away, but her legs gripped him ferociously. He tried to get a blow to her sternum, but she took his wrist and broke it as if it were the easiest thing in the world.

Sweet Mama of Shit, she was going to kill him good.

His head fell back again, and he saw an upside-down door opening. Rote stood in the hallway. His face looked hard and dead either way up.

'What are you looking at, nigger?' Cazie screamed.

Her hands came for his neck. This would be it, he knew. Her Devil's Mask face came close to his, and she kissed his mouth as she twisted his head.

'Mama,' he tried to say.

He felt his vertebrae straining, then snapping like links in a chain, one after the other. The pain was not so bad.

As he slipped into the dark, he was dimly aware that he was coming again.

Luckily, there was a quadrangle on campus big enough to land a helicopter in. It attracted a crowd, but there were enough police around to cover that.

Lynch wore a plain black jumpsuit, with a flying jacket to conceal his shoulder-holstered Magnum. The shoulders of the jacket were padded asymmetrically to disguise the weapon. He strode through the police cordons, accompanied by the local man, Inspector Woolbridge. They had kept piping him updates through his earplug radio while he was airborne. He had done his best to ignore the details. He knew the basic situation, and he wanted to assess the specifics from the ground up.

'Anderton. I want to speak to Anderton.'

'Of course, sir,' said Woolbridge. Lynch hoped the policeman would prove a good investment.

'You have him?'

'He's here.'

He did not waste words on a reply. The police were standing around outside what he knew from the maps he had studied in the chopper to be the School of Chemistry. There were groups of students loitering, rubbernecking. Rumours would be all over the shop by now, no doubt about that.

'Woolbridge, we have to contain the spread of information. See to it.'

'Pardon?'

'Get these surplus personnel out of the way. I don't care how. Bomb threat. Declare this a high-risk AIDS-infected area. Just do it.'

The policeman scurried off to talk to his men. Lynch's own team should be here within the hour. UCC had the resources the situation called for, and the government contracts that would ensure them a free hand in deploying them. In the background, Lynch spotted the pair of armed officers he had requested. They were not doing anything particularly useful, but they were there, just in case. The cops would be out of it soon.

The UCC chopper circled the campus once, and withdrew. For the moment, Lynch was on his own.

Inside the building, there was a large irregular blood-stain on the tiling. It was like being home.

The police had let him in unopposed. That was sloppy, but it saved him time.

'Anderton?'

His voice echoed around the corridors. Of course, the place would have been evacuated. There was an answering shout. Lynch walked towards it.

Through several doors, he found a man he recognized

from his file. Dr Xavier Anderton, Head of Research on the Leo Project. UCC were using signs of the Zodiac this year. This should have been the Cancer Project, but someone in public relations had nixed that. Not that PR should have been overly bothered about the image of this sort of work. The whole point was that it should not have one.

'Lynch. You know what I do.'

'Indeed,' said Anderton, a reedy, youngish-looking nonentity. Lynch knew he should not underestimate the man. He had probably killed more people than Lynch in his time.

'I understand you have a situation here.

Anderton laughed bitterly. 'That's one way of putting it, Lynch.'

'Have you guesstimated the damage?'

'That's difficult. We have some lab animals at liberty, and some unidentified infectees.'

'What have they got?'

'We don't have a name for it. Batch 125 is as good as any.'

Lynch knew Anderton was near the edge. There were two other people in the room, who must be Carson and Finch. They were in no better shape. For a moment, Lynch considered terminating the expendables, but he knew that would have a psychologically damaging effect on Anderton. For the minute, he needed the scientist.

'Batch 125? What have you got on that?'

'Not much. It wasn't very promising. It doesn't do what it's supposed to . . .'

Finch came in, excited in spite of herself. 'But what it does might be interesting, Mr Lynch. It's not Leo exactly, but there might be a whole other line of research in it.'

Lynch waved a hand.

'Okay, okay. I don't want the advanced stuff. Give me the basics.'

Anderton picked up a petri dish. The agar jelly was discoloured, greyish.

'This is more or less Batch 125. We ought to label it 126, since it was cooked up after our initial session, but it is as near as dammit what we used the first time round.'

It did not look impressive, but Lynch knew that nothing did until it killed or cured you.

'It's a virus. Well, this is a virus. 125 certainly was when we shot it into the animals, but there's some evidence that it might have gone crystalline on us in the system. It does different things to different subjects, seemingly at random.'

'Symptoms?'

'Total cellular trauma, in one case. Accelerated growth and vitality in another. The only constant seems to be increased aggression, and even then you have the choice of directing it inward or outward.'

'Can humans catch it?'

'We don't even know if it's a disease, Lynch, but for your purposes I think we have to assume they can.'

'If you don't know it's a disease, I'm assuming you haven't even thought about a cure?'

Anderton did not look happy. 'As you know, UCC gave us some parameters to work in. Leo is supposed to be virulent in the extreme, resistant to all forms of counter-treatment. We seem to have been able to lick that part of the problem.'

'So it can kill us but we can't kill it, eh? Congratulations, that must be a miracle of science.'

'I don't think you're being fair,' said Finch. 'We were working to specifics . . .'

'. . . just obeying orders, I know. Me too, Miss Finch. Now you've spilled something, and I have to mop it up. That's the way it goes.'

'Who did you take machismo lessons from, Lynch? Clint Eastwood? Rutger Hauer?'

He slapped her, hard. She was surprised.

'Caught you, didn't I, Miss Finch?'

She sobbed twice, then got herself under control.

'As you probably know, this is serious. The police are involved, but their part will soon be over. UCC have a team coming. Dr Anderton, you'll get whatever you want. You have the best facilities possible here, and I understand they're pulling some people off Aries and Libra to back you up. I just hope something good comes out of this. If there are any casualties, we've got rooms in the University Infirmary at our disposal. Now, I've got to go and make the Vice-Chancellor eat shit. I want you to know that this is a genuine fuckup, and I'd like you to think only in terms of damage limitation, you understand?'

He left them to it. Some people had no idea.

Robyn Askew was detailed to make breakfast. She was a veggie, but Rote, who admitted that human beings were carnivorous animals, insisted she cook him up a panful of bacon. Best breakfast in the world, the British fry-up. Five or six rashers of streaky, a couple of burst-yolk eggs, some optional button mushrooms, half a tomato grilled to a hot lump, and a slice of deep-fat-fried bread, with ketchup and strong tea. Robyn might get broody about it and Dave Higgitt was with her – a vegan who refused dairy products and any food so much as scraped against an animal – but Doug Templeton was on his side. Even if he had not been, Rote would have outvoted the others. Ever since he went underground, his unit had been under his total command. It was the only way.

Higgitt was spinning the tuner on the radio, trying to catch all the local and national news bulletins. It was unlikely they would make the BBC, but the independent local station ought to carry a report. Rote almost wanted them to have been identified. Eventually, when he was well out of the area, he would issue a statement claiming responsibility. Since putting out the eyes of the Duke of Bastardfordshire or whatever he called himself, the cell had not had a decent follow-up action. He was glad that there had been a chance to cause injury. The media always ignored actions that did not cause injury.

'Where's Chocolate Charlie?' Rote asked. The black youth – too dangerous and broody by half, he thought – was missing.

Templeton stabbed this thumb up towards the ceiling, and licked his lips.

'Poking Cazie,' he said through a grin. 'She likes her meat dark.'

That was typical of the unreal little slut. Rote knew from the first she was not serious about the cause. She was in it for weird kicks. Weird fucks. Cazie was a dilettante debutante. He knew the type. They oohed and ahhed over cuddly-wuddly ickle-wickle cutesy furry animally-poohs, and copped out when it came to an action.

Cazie had fucked up last night. She had been as much use as a bad case of genital warts. And her tagalongs had been no better. Thommy and Clare.

Higgitt turned off the radio, disgusted. Cazie and Derm were making a lot of noise. Templeton laughed, and Robyn looked disgusted.

Rote had had to make do with Clare, but he had really wanted to pour the pork to Cazie. It was just that he knew he could take Thommy, but he was not sure of Derm. He could win in a fight, but there would *be* a fight. Thommy was a spineless piss-heart, and had backed down with a shit-eating smile at the first sign of real pain. Derm might have required more sweat and bruising.

Next, Rote would try for a major coup. An action against a zoo, or a circus. Maybe Cruft's or the Horse of the Year Show. People were hurting animals all the time, and he ached to hurt them back.

The noise upstairs was ridiculous. At first, Rote thought Cazie was just a screamer. Then he realized it was Derm who was screaming.

'Shit,' he said.

The four of them jammed the stairs together, and jogged up towards the landing, towards the nerve-scraping screams.

As Eddie Zero woke up, he fumbled on his bedside for a cassette from his shoebox, and slotted it into his deck. He could not get up without rock 'n' roll. It was The Coasters, 'Poison Ivy'.

The music got to him, and he rolled out of his single bed. He sat in his vest and Y-fronts on the edge of the bed, and looked around his Hall of Residence room. A life-size Elvis poster sneered at him from the back of his door.

He stumbled over to the wash-basin, and splashed cold water on his face, wiping the wet into his greasy hair, shaping his quiff. He skipped shaving, but took the trouble to sluice out his mouth with soapy water, forcing it between his teeth. He was out of toothpaste.

The Coasters got onto 'Bad Blood'.

He supposed he had resigned from Campus Radio yesterday. He remembered telling Posie Columba what she could do with the middle of Friday nights.

He took out his drainpipes and forced himself into them, sucking in his stomach to tighten the belt. He tied his bootlace tie in the collar of his knife-point collar-tip paisley shirt, and got into his embroidered waistcoat. At least he was looking like something.

'Yakkety-Yak.'

There was a scratching at his door, and he wondered

who it could be. Nobody ever bothered him on campus. Unless it was some snotnose wanting to borrow milk.

And why couldn't they just knock, for the sake of Carl Perkins?

He opened the door, and there was no one in the corridor. The scratching, he realized had been at the bottom of the door.

He looked down, and saw a rabbit nestling on his pink-socked feet.

'Riot in Cell Block Number Nine'.

Rote was out of the way by the time Cazie got to the door. He was quick. She would have to stretch herself to get him.

His top soldier was not so well prepared. Rote had slammed past him, pushing him against a wall. Cazie saw exposed throat and reached for it. Flesh parted like overcooked pasta, and she grabbed a fistful of tendons and nerves.

Holding the man as if by his shirt collar, she whipped him around, and swung him into the wall. She let go and he crumpled.

She was still hungry, and there was bacon frying below. She looked at the knotty red mess in the dead man's throat and was tempted.

But there was no time for that. She had three more people to take care of before breakfast. She knew now how much better than them she was.

She also needed a bath and clothes, but this business was bound to be messy, so for the time being she just put on her old dressing gown. It was already torn and bloody, so more mess would not matter.

Downstairs, where they had retreated, they were talking about her. Rote was the dangerous one. She would go for him first.

But Rote was clever. He sent his other man upstairs for her, with a jemmy. The weapon, of course, was already blooded.

She remembered the sound she had heard when Rote had hit the security guard last night. It was a good sound.

Excited, she squared off against the man in the hallway. He paused, put off by the sight of his comrade gurgling his last, and began to swing the jemmy in calculated arcs before him.

She was cool, and did not hiss and claw the air.

'Girlie, you're dead.'

With lamentable slowness, he jabbed the jemmy at her like a sword. She just reached out and took it.

'Do you want to see some magic?' she asked.

She bent the jemmy into an oval, but it cracked at the top and spoiled the effect. She threw it at the man as he came for her, and raised a blood-filled bruise on his forehead.

He covered his head with his hands, but she had him anyway.

Cazie kicked out, and snapped the rail off the top of the banisters. The landing was lined with jagged wooden pickets. She took Rote's man by his elbows and forced him backwards, down onto the spikes. Three came up through him, bringing dark squirts of blood and trails of offal. His arms came away from his face as his eyes filled up with the red stuff. She kissed him, not like she had kissed Derm, but out of friendliness. He was dead now and could not do her any harm.

'I'm coming down now, Rote. Ready or not!'

Giggling like a girl, she tripped past the dead people and went down the stairs. Her back teeth hurt, as if they were just coming through. She knew who she was now.

The woman was no problem. Cazie just hugged her to death. Her back snapped like a breadstick. Cazie left her in the kitchen, and went looking for Rote in the Action Room.

The light was off down there, and Cazie could hear him in the dark. She could hear things she had never heard before. The whisper of breath, the beating of a heart, the slightest rustle of cloth.

She paused at the head of the stairs, and brought her thumbnail up to her mouth. It was tougher than she thought, and she could not chew it. She nicked her tongue, and tasted her own blood. It gave her a cocaine rush, and she had to steady herself.

Rote came for her while she was off balance, grabbing her ankles and pulling her downstairs. Her spine jolted as she slammed against every step. She felt a series of forceful blows to the chest as she lay prone on the stairs. She did not lose her wind, but she was dizzy.

She realized she could see in the dark now. Rote was bent over her, teeth bared like a cartoon monster. It was almost funny.

He held her down with a knee in her stomach, and ripped her robe open. His hand came down as fast as even she could move, and he had her by the throat. She knew it was no use snarling at him. He would not be impressed.

'Now, bitch,' he said, 'we play my games.'

'Fuck you, Rote!'

'No, Cazie, fuck *you*!'

Then he was on her.

The convoy of unmarked trucks was two hours out of an indeterminate-looking site in South London. Private-Equivalent Willard Longendyke had no idea where he was being deployed, and did not much care.

He had other priorities. Like the Need. Like the three

highly unauthorized, non-regulation-issue needles in his inside top pocket.

The men in the back of his truck sat quiet, checking their weapons and the seals on their suits. There was none of that camaraderie shit in the teams, with everyone whistling 'Colonel Bogey' or talking about the folks back home.

If you were in the Covert Security Division, chances were you were the brand of dude the folks back home did not miss that much.

Sergeant-Equivalent Bosworth, the Bozz Man, was walking up and down the truck, steadying himself by getting hand-holds on the hanging ropes, performing one of his interminable snap inspections.

Longendyke would pass. He was careful about shit like that. He had to be.

The backs of his hands had been crawling for hours, though. His missing pill was phantom throbbing.

He always got that way when he was close to the Need.

Fuckin' Panama.

It had been enough to give anybody the Need. A couple of rounds in his leg and one missing testicle were adequately qualified to jack up the pain level beyond belief, and when Sergeant Gomez Gomez came around with a sweet little package of sugar to take all the nasties away, the way ahead had been clear. Just ease into a big blue vein and depress the plunger, and liquid dynamite squirts all round your body, giving you the biggest all-over hard-on you ever experienced.

The first time he flew, in the Canal Zone foxhole, he had jerked off until his remaining ball was dry and shrivelled as a raisin. He knew not what cocktail of meth, H and coke Gomez Gomez had cooked up in his home brew, but it sure made jacking off into a lifetime-experience. A couple more jabs like that, and he would pick up milkmaid's wrist, or whatever repetitive stress injury you could get from, as they say in the Yew Kay, wanking like the clappers.

Since then, he had been onto the shit like Wile E. Coyote onto the menu in a Kentucky Fried Road Runner restaurant.

This gig had come up suddenly, and his beeper had beeped while he was making his connection. That had nearly queered the deal, but Merv the Medicine Man knew who his best customers were. Longendyke had even concluded the hand-over before reporting to the Bozz Man.

That was a mercy. Otherwise, he would have been crawling the walls before the teams were in the field. That might get noticed. Once he had his jab, he would be okay. The situation would become a cool breeze. He always liked to fly into the field. It had not got him killed yet. In the Zone, he had heard a brasshat say that some of the best Medal of Honour winners were stoned to the gills when they did their guts and glory thing.

Next to Longendyke, Tripps tried on his filter faceplate, pulling his hood around it. These Zombie outfits were guaranteed against radiation, infection, herpes, measles, BSE and the Black Death. In the teams, they were called 'all-over rubbers'.

He wondered if the Lynch-Mob would be top dog on this operation. That Brit was one scary officer. Longendyke had been under him at a terrorist gig in the Med. Lynch had gone Rambo and cleaned up a whole nest of towelheads by himself. None of the hostages had come out alive, but the stuff that counted – UCC papers or some shit like that – had been turned over neatly to the company suits.

The Bozz Man looked him over, and went on to Tripps.

Longendyke's non-ball was a blob of pain in his groin. He kept shifting his seat, but it was no good. The Need was hotting up.

Fuckin' Panama.

With TWA and Pan-Am and that instantaneous matter transmission device everyone *knew* the goddamn Government bought up and hid away from the public use, who in the name of Johnny Carson's sister's black cat's ass needed a goddamn canal anyway.

Just a groove in the ground with mud and water and ships in it. Shit, was all. Shit, shit, shit . . .

He had been tagged as a casualty while he was in the latrine. Fuckin' crapper exploded under him. They never found his surplus *cojone*. Everybody said sorry. Even the Prezz sent a sorry telegram. But sorry had not cut the cocaine. Sorry and a flag-waving procession had meant a damn sight less than the massive pay hike UCC offered veterans who did not ask questions. He was fresh out of patriotic zeal and, besides, his Need was getting real expensive and the salary cheque kept his connections happy.

He had never been to England before, and so that was a trip in itself. The CDS was a supra-national outfit with sites in London, Marseilles, New York State, San Bernardino, Rio de Janeiro, Johannesberg, Hong Kong, Canberra, Malmo, Prague, Osaka and the Antarctic. UCC was registered as a Bahaman corporation for tax purposes, but its head offices were London, New York and Tokyo. Despite his designer cockney accent, Josh Unwin was an American citizen.

'Shape up,' the Bozz Man shouted as the truck jumped a bit, obviously rolling off the regular road.

'Remember, this is not an assault. You will take your positions with no discharge of weapons. There will be a parcel of civs in the vicinity, and you are not unduly to throw a fright into them.'

Everyone nodded. Tripps pulled off his mask, and let it hang at his throat.

The truck rolled to a halt, and the Bozz Man threw back the doors.

The team got out in an orderly fashion, and assembled for inspection. The other trucks, six of them, were parked in a row, their complements lining up outside.

He realized they were on a college campus. Young people with books were watching the team assemble. There were buildings all around, and trees and lawns.

Longendyke's skin reacted badly to the sunlight. As he straightened up, blinking, adjusting to the new environment, he desperately wanted to creep off somewhere and have his jab.

He saw the Lynch-Mob looming out of a building, trailing civilian cops. The Bozz Man and all the other NCO-equivalents lined up to lick ass and salute. Lynch passed out orders, and Longendyke knew just from the feel of the place that there would be blood spilled. He could always tell as soon as his boots hit the turf.

Right now, it was a stroll in the park. Later, it would be a hell on earth. The Need was constant, eating him away inside, gnawing at his brain. The needles were burning a hole under his Zombie suit.

Rote was going to make the bitch pay for Templeton, Higgitt and Robyn Askew. And for fucking up a simple raid.

She was strong, no doubt about that. Stronger than she should be, but she could not hope to match him.

In the army, when he was a kid, he had discovered wrestling. Not the namby-pamby showoff stuff costumed clowns got up to on Saturday afternoons on the telly, but the hard, fast, high-contact sport that went back to Ancient Greece. They had kicked him off the squad for breaking too many arms, and out of the army for selling not-yet-surplus equipment.

Since then, he had had the Cause. He hated people a lot, and he had no qualms about smashing them down if they were Evil.

Cazie was Evil, no doubt about that.

Killing her was not enough. She had to be broken first. Humbled.

She broke his hold, and twisted under him, but he whipped his arms under hers and got a full nelson, his knotted fists pressing her head flat against a stair. He got his knee in the small of her back.

To do what he had to do to her, he would have to free his hands long enough to unbuckle his belt and wriggle out of his jeans. That would give her a chance.

He let her head up, and hammered it down again. She did not say anything, but her body remained taut beneath him, not relaxed. She was not out. He hit her head against the stair again. And again. And again.

She was losing it, he could tell. There was blood all over the place. He had probably roughed up her face. That did not matter. He was not going to rape her because she was pretty.

Rote slipped his arms free and undid his belt. He pulled it out of his jeans, and held it up in one fist like a bullwhip. It might come in handy. Then he dropped his denims. He had had a hard on since he had first grabbed Cazie by the ankles.

The bitch was going to take it every way he could think of, and he could think of plenty.

Groggily, Cazie raised herself on her elbows, and turned her head to look up at him. There was blood on her face, but he could not see any disfiguring wound. Shame.

He lashed out with his belt, and caught her across the shoulders. It did not stop her moving. She rolled over onto her back, and wiped her bloody fringe out of her eyes.

'Do you feel like a man, Rote?'

He did not answer.

'Like a great big bull of a man?'

She touched her breasts with her hands, leaving red smears like zebra-stripes. Her ribs shifted as she breathed.

The fight had gone out of her. All she had left was words.

'Come on and rape me then, Tarzan. Let's see if you've got the dick for it.'

He whipped her again, three times crosswise.

Then she caught the belt, and tugged. He fell forwards onto her, his body on hers.

He pulled his arm back to deliver a blow . . .

. . . but she had him by the testicles.

'Let's see if you've got the . . .'

She pushed his chest hard, forcing him away from her, but her other hand still gripped hard.

'. . . BALLS!'

There was a white-hot sunburst of agony between his legs, and he felt his bowels letting go.

She was flinging him across the room as easily as he had flung the rabbit away last night.

He hit the corkboard and collapsed.

His vision was messed up now. Lines of purple and orange squiggled on the surface of his eyes. He was emptying through a hole in his groin. He felt himself sinking.

'What's the matter, Tarzan? Want your dick back?'

She stood over him now, bending close, her breath on his face. She touched him, touched his throat, his chin, forcing his jaws open.

Then she pushed her fistful of meat into his mouth, and he could not breathe any more.

He knew she was watching him die.

* * *

85

Sparks was in the Infirmary, Monica was 'in a meeting', and Brian was in a dilemma.

From what Sparks's sidekick at Security had told him, things were likely to get serious. His old boozing buddy was down with a skull fracture, possible brain damage, and some weird kind of throat wound. Someone had given him a major bashing with the proverbial blunt instrument, and – after that – something else had had a good go at ripping (*chewing?*) his windpipe out.

Brian had tried to get through to Monica, but her V-P was running interference for her. He thought back for a while to the days when he had written a pamphlet entitled 'Fuck the Establishment' and seriously talked about fire-bombing US Army bases, and knew he could not keep this quiet. He would have to rat on Monica's Animal Lib friends. There was no rabbit alive worth killing a man for.

He could not go straight to the police – after all, he was going to want to cover his arse on 'lending' Cazie the keys. That meant he had to see Jackson.

Ernest Jackson, the Vice-Chancellor of the University, was a wet liberal from way back. Brian had always thought him a decent man. Even when the students felt the need to burn him in effigy he had kept his sense of humour. But, deep down, Brian knew the V-C was a quivering civil servant who would preserve his position at the expense of anything.

This was going to be a mess.

And Jackson was keeping him waiting. Brian had not even worked up any interest in flirting with Gabrielle, Jackson's stunning receptionist, and none of the academic journals in his reception room took his fancy. He had to restrain himself from pacing up and down like an expectant father. In Jackson's office, he could hear the drone of light conversation, punctuated by cheerful laughs. Brian imagined V-C exchanging quips and brandies with some venerable professor as they worked out seating plans for a testimonial dinner, or decided on the cover design of the new University prospectus.

'Any idea how long?' he asked.

Gabrielle looked up from her blood-red nails, and tapped her file against heart-shaped lips.

'It could be a while. He dithers a lot, you know.'

'I know.'

Gabrielle went back to her talons. She was giving them an edge.

'I saw a rabbit on campus this morning,' she said.

'Oh really?'

'Yes. It must be summer at last.'

He did not care about rabbits. Rabbits in the Chem Building. Rabbits in Jason's room.

Rabbits!

He should have guessed. No wonder Jason's bunny looked so messed up. He had resisted Jason's demands that the thing be buried, and put it in a twist-tie rubbish bag. It was out for the refuse people to pick up, in one of the neat row of bins outside the neat row of faculty cottages at the far edge of the campus.

It probably was not important, but when he got through with Jackson he ought to cut class and take Jason to the Infirmary and get his bite looked at. There was a slim chance of infection.

Jackson's door opened, and the V-C showed Professor Prawer out with much hand-shaking and joviality.

'Hello, Brian,' he said, 'sorry to keep you on hold. We've got a graduation ceremony to stage manage. Prawer's trying to convince me to lay on a laser hologram spectacle.'

Prawer left laughing, and Brian wondered where to start with the bad news.

'Could you wait just a teensy minute-ette more, Brian. Gaby, any word from the police about the unpleasantness in Chem?'

87

Gabrielle shook her head.

'That's what I want to talk to you about, Ernest. Sparks . . .'

'I appreciate your concern, Brian. It's a bad thing. I hope it doesn't get blown up by the press. The police think it was some student desperately trying to get drugs . . .'

'I think I have some infor – '

'Terrible business, drugs. I'd thought we'd got that problem under control since last year. The counselling service is supposed to be first-rate.'

'It wasn't drugs, it was the animals.'

'Yes, animals, animals. It's tragic. Young people sinking that low.'

'No . . .'

Someone came into the room.

'Jackson.'

Brian and the V-C stopped talking. The newcomer was a mutilated Adonis with a Michael Heseltine hairstyle. He was dressed in some sort of quasi-military set-up. Gabrielle dropped her file.

'Frank Lynch, UCC.'

The V-C extended a hand, and Lynch took it in what must be a bone-crushing grip. Brian thought he saw something that might be a gun under the man's jacket as he pumped Jackson's arm.

'I was told you were coming,' Jackson said, wrung out. 'You have all the cooperation I can give.'

'Great. Let's go in your office and talk cases. The rest of my team will be here, soon. I'd like as little panic as possible. It'll be your responsibility to keep your student body under control . . .'

The men disappeared into Jackson's office. Brian stood outside like a spare prick as the door was shut in his face.

'Shit!'

Gabrielle had her file again, and was trying to look phlegmatic.

'Don't tell me,' Brian said, 'this isn't England any more. This is El Fucking Salvador.'

Jason must be getting that cereal that puts energy into kids for breakfast, lunch, tea and supper. After four hours with the boy, Abigail felt thirty years older.

Fresh from humiliating her at frisbee-throwing, he had taken her indoors and persuaded her to be a monster. She had chased him up and down stairs and in and out of cupboards and wardrobes, hissing through orange peel Dracula fangs, while he had shot at her with his plastic raygun. No wonder the good guys always came out on top in science fiction films. If Jason was representative of the average space cadet, there were no monsters in the universe who could hope to keep up with him, let alone overtake, disable and devour him.

Abigail felt secure in the knowledge that the universe was kept peaceful by the likes of Jason Connors.

Her immediate problem was slowing the boy down long enough for her to make them dinner. Brian had left her some canned beans and sliced bread – typical man food – in the kitchen, and she hoped to make it palatable by adding some herbs and a pinch of curry powder.

But Jason clung to her waist, firing death rays off in every direction, and she needed to keep a hold on his arm in order to stop him having her eye out, or doing himself some damage.

She swore never to have children. Not that that was likely. She was a brain, and a virgin. They would not serve her in pubs, and automatically offered her half price in cinemas and on buses. Only a pervert would be interested in her.

She had heard that Brian Connors was a pervert, but

that was from a girl who had dropped out of his American Cinema course. That must be difficult, not having the intellect to grasp the subtleties of a John Wayne movie. Abigail thought Brian was quite attractive in an elderly sort of way, but he had practically given her sweeties this morning.

It was tough having an IQ of 156, and a body that would not grow up. Perhaps she should dress more glamorously, in vampish slit skirts and scarlet lipstick. She would probably end up looking like the winner of a primary school fancy dress contest.

'Jason, could you let go? I have to cook.'

The little creature clung on tenaciously.

'Careful, you'll spoil my skirt. It's only thin.'

Jason growled and laughed.

'Get off, don't be silly.'

'Can we play monsters some more?'

'You have to eat first, Jason. Even monsters have to eat, and space cadets.'

Jason reluctantly released her from his deathgrip, and stood to attention. He gave the Masters of the Universe Sign of Power.

'Can I help cook?'

Abigail was doubtful. She had a mental image flash of a kitchen after a chainsaw massacre, with gouts of ketchup splashed like an action painting on the walls, and beans squashed against the windowpanes. But she ought to delegate something non-dangerous to him, to keep his hands busy while she got things ready.

'Do you know how to open tins, Jason?'

He looked unsure, then smiled and nodded vigorously. She handed him a can of beans, and pulled out drawers in search of an opener.

But before she found the right drawer, Jason had the can open. She could not be sure, but she thought he had just traced a circle on the top with his thumbnail, pressing down slightly. Then, he had pulled the top up with his fingers and neatly disposed of the tin circle in the wastebin.

'That was neat, Jason.'

'Can I do it again?'

'Sure. Here's the other tin.'

Jason smiled, licking the tomato sauce off his thumb. The streamlined telephone began burping.

Monica wished she had not shouted at Lindy. It was not her fault Monica had not told her to let Brian talk to her.

She tried Brian's home number, but the girl there – not Debbie, another one, she realized with irritation – said he was invigilating, which she knew to be not true. She tried his department, but they had no ideas. He had said he would be in the Union Building about lunch time. But when was that – twelve? one? two?

Berenice kept an eye on the developing situation. There were rumours of armed men in white decontamination suits around the Chem Building, and one of the switchboard girls had overheard that the guard in the Infirmary had been savaged by some kind of wild animal.

She could not concentrate on the business she was supposed to take care of, and just dumped all her correspondence in the 'In' tray for future reference. She was wondering who to phone next when Brian showed up. Luckily, Lindy let him in.

'Bad news. Your Cazie put a friend of mine in a hospital bed.'

'I know that.'

'There's more. UCC have sent someone down to look into the mess. I've met it, and I don't think it's friendly.'

'What?'

'A gorilla called Lynch. He's browbeating Jackson as

91

we speak. He's not your average corporation man either. He carries what looks to be an extremely large gun.'

'Jackson can't let a fucking gunslinger loose on campus.'

'Jackson doesn't have a whole lot to say about it. Listen, I'm not supposed to talk about this, but I've been blabbing about lots of secrets recently. UCC are heavily into the University. Josh Unwin would like us to name a building or two after him. A gymnasium or an art gallery or something friendly like that. I know from the funding papers that have to come through the department. UCC have got a lot of government contracts, and, as you know, the government gives us our charter.'

'But UCC are a pharmaceuticals company . . .'

'The Unscrupulous Chemical Company, we used to call them.'

'. . . what could they want with the Humanities Department?'

'Psychological stuff. Scary stuff. It's probably Ministry of Defence-funded, in the end. Everything bloody else is.'

Monica was not happy at all. Pictures were forming in her mind that she did not like.

'Defence, shit. We all know what that means.'

'Uh huh. I preferred it when it was called the Ministry of War. That was more honest.'

Monica's intercom buzzed. It had to be important for Lindy and Bern to let the call through.

'Hello?'

'Jackson for you,' came Bern's distorted voice.

'Jackson?'

'The V-C, remember?'

'Yeah, put him on.' She looked at Brian. He shrugged.

'Miss Flint, Monica . . .'

She was no judge of character over the telephone, but she had to talk to Ernest Jackson four or five times a week.

He was usually condescending, patronizing and paternal. Now, he sounded like a man reeling from eighteen rounds of intellectual boxing with Bernard Levin.

'. . . we have to talk. Are you free?'

'Free? Sure. What is it, Ernest?'

Usually he winced when she used his first name. This time he swallowed it, and carried on.

'You understand we have some problems today?'

'The police are all over the place. Yes.'

'It seems . . . um . . . that it's more serious than we thought at first . . . for the safety of . . . for all our sakes . . . we're going to have to institute some precautions . . .'

'What sort of precautions?'

'. . . um . . . er . . .'

She could imagine him with his hand over the receiver, turning to get instructions from someone in his office. This was new.

'There's someone with him,' she told Brian, 'pulling the strings.'

'Lynch.'

'Maybe.'

Jackson was back. 'Stringent precautions, I'm afraid. We're setting up roadblocks at the main entrance. No one will be allowed on or off the campus . . .'

'What? You cannot be serious!'

'. . . um . . . er . . .'

'You can't just lock seven thousand people up like that.'

'I . . .'

'Jackson, what *is* going on?'

There was a fumbling on the other end of the line, and a new voice came on.

'Miss Flint, my name is Frank Lynch. I'm here representing Unwin Chemicals. We've been funding the facility that was breached last night.'

'I know a bit about that.'

'Good, then I'm sure you'll understand when I say we have to impose a strict quarantine. Some animals escaped last night. I don't know how, and I'm not particularly interested. But these weren't just rabbits. They were experimental subjects . . .'

Monica's heart stopped. Then started again.

She did not want to ask the next question, afraid that Lynch would give her a straight answer.

She steadied herself. 'What have they got?'

'We can't say at the moment.'

'Crap! You'll have to say something soon. Plague? Herpes? Some kind of biological warfare bug?'

'Nothing like that. We're developing vaccines, not viruses. But there is a potential for infection. I'm not a scientist, I don't know the polysyllables. It'll be two days, maximum. That's the incubation period. If it's all over, then we can go home. Mr Jackson is busy setting up dormitories for those staff and students who are not resident on campus. Let's not make a drama out of a crisis, Miss Flint!'

'Okay, okay, okay. But if you want me to sell this to the students, you'll have to give me some guarantees.'

'Such as?'

'Such as *no fucking guns*, for a start. I'll get you volunteers to man any roadblocks or perimeter patrols you need . . .'

'That should be acceptable. The only armed personnel we have are out in the woods hunting rabbits. I'm sure you understand.'

'Put Jackson back. We have to square a meeting.'

Cazie enjoyed driving. She took a long detour on her trip from town to the campus, just so she could open up the little MG her father had given her and push its engine to the limits. She had never got the needle up higher than 70 before, and now seemed to be as good a time as any to find out how fast the machine could go.

It should have been difficult, twisting through country lanes at nearly 100 miles per hour, but Cazie knew she could do it. She could feel the roads in front of her, knew what the other cars would do before they did it, and had supreme confidence in her ability to survive anything.

She had cleaned up, of course, before leaving the house. She had had to take a thorough bath to get all the blood off. Examining her face in the mirror, she could not see anything apart from a few faint white lines to mark the cuts she had got. She had torn a blouse up the back trying to put it on, and realized she would have to be careful.

Sometimes, she did not know her own strength.

Dressed in tight jeans and a loose sweater, she had taken a tour of the house. It was a shame about Derm, but that could not be helped. She had left him on the bed upstairs, but arranged him peacefully with a sheet over him. She felt desire just touching him, but suppressed it. Derm had been her friend, her lover. Using him now would be disgusting.

Besides there had been Rote, and the others. She had put them all in the Action Room. The one on the stairs had had to be pulled free, and he was still transfixed by a broken banister.

When she had finished moving them, the desire was too powerful to fight. Her palate ached, and her stomach squirmed. The bacon in the pan in the kitchen had shrivelled to black curls, leaving the smell of burned meat smoking through the house. Carefully, she had turned off the gas and thrown away the ruined rashers.

It had had to be the woman, of course. Cazie thought the men might be too tough, too stringy. She considered cooking but there did not appear to be a need.

She had got the body up on a table, sliced her pullover open with a nail, and had breakfast.

She knew better than to make a mess now, and had sucked the blood out of the mouthfuls of flesh before tearing them loose with her teeth and swallowing them.

Dimly, as she feasted, she remembered another girl, another Cazie. A girl who had been afraid to do anything, afraid of her Daddy, afraid even of her friends. She was gone now, as if she were a dream to be forgotten upon awakening.

Eating then, driving now, Cazie knew she was the *real* girl.

A rabbit darted out of the hedgerow forty or fifty yards ahead. It was a simple matter of three or four degrees of turn on the wheel, just a flicker of pressure on the accelerator.

She got the animal dead on. She did not stop to see, but she knew she had neatly squashed its middle, leaving the head and the back legs whole.

'Rabbit ain't got no tail at all,' she hummed to herself, 'tail at all, tail at all. Rabbit ain't got no tail at all . . .'

110. That was as fast as the speedometer could register.

'. . . just a powder PUFF!'

The trees, road signs, houses, fences, hedges, telegraph poles flew past like bullets. She had dented the bumper and bonnet a couple of times, but did not give a shit.

The wind hit her face, parted and sliced around her head as if she was the prow of a ship. She smelled things she had never been able to make out before. She opened her mouth to catch flies, to eat the air. The atmosphere itself was delicious.

Briefly, she was in the throes of an orgasm. She had become used to them by now. Her hands did not waver on the wheel.

A car turned unexpectedly into the road from a blind corner, but she had *known* it was coming, and that the

96

driver would not have the guts to keep coming. The fucker was in a ditch before he knew it.

She thought about stopping and finishing him, but he was a quarter of a mile back by then, and there would always be others.

Cazie had had enough driving. She had things to do on campus. She did the tightest-ever U-turn, and was on her way again.

Longendyke was on perimeter patrol. And the Bozz Man had stuck with him some student dipshit called Barry Bewes, who kept asking questions he knew he had better not even think of answering.

The Need was overpowering. He stood rigidly to attention, fists clenched in his gauntlets, teeth gritted.

He wished he still had his gun. At least that would have been something to hold.

Barry kept yammering and jabbering, a white noise background.

He could feel the needles in his breast pocket, safe in cigar tubes, snug against his tit.

They were in a residential area of the college. Beyond the lines of student flats was an empty field.

The Bozz Man told him the Lynch-Mob wanted the campus population contained, and so they were enforcing quarantine. They were also on a naturewatch field trip and if they saw any rabbits they were to report in. Barry thought that was funny, but Longendyke knew nothing the Bozz Man said was funny.

He was sweating with the Need, burning with the Need.

He considered sighting an invisible rabbit and sending Barry off to make a report. He could claim that his headset mike was down. Then, when the limpdick was legging around, he could slip between the houses and administer the home remedy in a minute.

97

Then he would be flying solo.

Still, the Bozz Man was a bigger boogey than the Need. He would have to tough it out.

'Look at that,' Barry said, pointing.

Someone stumbled out of the nearest house, bleeding from the mouth and nose.

'That's Preston, from the Infirmary, one of the nurses.'

When Barry looked back, he had his faceplate up and in position. It cut out some of the noise.

The bleeder fell to his knees and Longendyke could swear that his head was expanding.

It was. This was no shitdream.

Nurse Preston's cheeks inflated like a football, and his forehead bulged. White stretches of scalp showed in his hair. The neck expanded, and rips grew under the now-tiny-seeming ears. Panicked eyes shrank in gaping sockets. Seams appeared in his skin, and parted, showing red and muscle. The flesh swelled around his nose, making the protuberance an indentation.

Then Preston's head exploded.

Lynch thought he had things under control, but Anderton knew different.

The CSD man had his back-up team deployed effectively, even if their guns were locked in their trunks. He had spread them around the campus, each one tagged with a student volunteer to keep them in line. Anderton knew how little provocation it would take for Lynch to order his men to get rid of their encumbrances.

Anderton had run every test he could get together at short notice on 126. Outside the body, it was a pushover – a few degrees temperature change either way, and it was dead mould. But inside, it was an unpredictable little bugger, and he would have to jab up another bunch of animals to have even a chance at guessing what it would do.

Finch had tabulated five or six possible reactions, none of them good. Lynch was not interested yet. Give him a few infectees, and he would start asking for treatment scenarios. Anderton knew the UCC man would be happier with a rifle in his hands than a hypodermic syringe.

Lynch had not had time to listen to the lecture Anderton had prepared, the one that began, '125 isn't exactly a disease, it's supposed to be a symbiote. In some ways, once you catch it, you could be *better* than you were before . . .'

The CSD man had left a suited guard, Tripps, to look after the team in the lab. Anderton wondered if he were there to keep externals away, or to make sure they stayed at their benches.

Anderton had a pain at the back of his neck from bending over too many microscopes, and he knew he was more likely to find a cure for cancer than deal with his dandruff. Since he had signed up with UCC and put himself in the supertax bracket, his life had been going down the plughole. The corporation was a lot like a virus in the way it acted on people – it got into your system, took it over completely, sucked out whatever it wanted, and left you behind as a pile of compost.

Once, at a reception, he had been within twelve seats of Josh Unwin. That was supposed to be an honour. Anderton thought the corporate head a vulgar publicity-seeker, and knew he was just the figurehead for a cabal of faceless boardroom plutocrats. Unwin was always off breaking land-speed records and appearing on television quiz shows. Meanwhile, the juggernaut of UCC rolled onwards, crushing anyone who got under its killer wheels. And UCC only provided a service. It had no use for Leo itself, it just had a client who dreamed up the specifics and made a commission. Anderton knew exactly the kind of people who would be the corporation's clients on a project like this.

There was a chance, of course. If only 125 could kill the rabbits before they could pass it on.

If only . . .

Then the Infirmary called up, and told him about the three kids from York House. Thomas Ward, Clare Moyle, Peter Aston.

Then more reports came in.

125 was starting to get busy.

The Zombies would not let Brian and Monica into the unmarked lorry the UCC team were using as a field HQ, but Lynch came out to see them.

'Miss Flint, thank you for your cooperation,' he said, ignoring Brian as he had done in Jackson's office. 'You've been a great help. In these situations, panic can be as dangerous as a disease.'

How many of these 'situations' had Lynch been in?

'What's going on at the Infirmary?' Monica demanded. Brian was impressed by her single-mindedness. 'Why won't your people let us see the patients?'

'Risk of infection. Your Dr Hind made the decision.'

'But you're enforcing it?'

Lynch did not even look annoyed, although Monica's tart tone made her opinion clear. When you looked like Frank Lynch, Brian supposed, you did not have to register anger to be imposing. Against his will, he could not help but be fascinated by the criss-cross scars on the man's cheeks and neck. He had either been clawed by a lion or processed through a hay-baler. Brian bet the cat or the machine that had done it was in much worse shape than Lynch.

The man made a gesture of exasperation – oddly actorish, as if it was just an excuse not to answer a tough question – and tried to come across as the world's most long-suffering small-town copper.

'Miss, I wish you'd stop thinking of us as an Occupation Force. We're here to help. There's a very great danger, and you'll only make things worse by treating us as if we were the Gestapo. We've gone out of our way to keep you, and the University authorities, informed.'

'Then, who . . .'

'Now, if you'll excuse me, we're very busy. If you could come by later, once we've sorted out where everybody is going to spend the night, I'll give you a complete update on the situation. Take care.'

Take care!

Lynch went back into his lorry, and Brian and Monica were left with a couple of the Zombies.

They wore white jumpsuits, sealed at the ankles and wrists so the boots and gauntlets were part of the uniform. Balaclava hoods hung behind their necks. Brian knew if they added atmosphere-filtration masks with faceplates, they would look even scarier. Now, they only had expressionless faces to hide behind.

'What now?' she asked.

'For me, Jason. I phoned in, and Abigail says he's okay, but I want to take a look myself.'

'Abigail?'

She was jealous.

'Just a babysitter. Who do you think I am, Warren Beatty?'

She thought of a clever answer, but threw it away unused. Brian saw she was too concerned with this chaos to keep up the wisecracks. That was good. This was serious.

Barry had got blood all over himself. At least the incident of the man with the Incredible Exploding Head had shut the kid up.

101

Now, Longendyke had been pulled from the perimeter. A couple of the medics had wrapped Barry up in a polythene bender and were carrying him between them like a shot leopard.

Someone was trying to talk to the student, trying to get a reaction out of him. In the sagging shroud, he looked as if he had been prematurely body-bagged.

Longendyke was a furnace inside. The Need, the needle . . .

As they trotted through the populated part of the campus, people got out of their way. Part of the CSD job was to radiate fuck-with-me-not vibes at all times.

The Bozz Man saw him, somehow recognized him through his mask and suit, and called him over.

'Report to the truck, Longendyke,' he said. 'Gail will want to check you out.'

Gail was the field surgeon.

'I feel fine, sir. These suits work real good.'

The Bozz Man growled. 'Just do it, Longendyke.'

There was a distraction, and Sergeant-Equivalent Bosworth had his pistol drawn. The pistol that was supposed to be in the truck.

Barry jack-knifed out of the carriers' hands, and was inch-worming across the grass. Two of the medics moon-hopped after him, but Longendyke got there first, coming down hard on the turdbreath's back. The student struggled and kicked, but his hands had been twist-tied with a plastic tag. He was having a shit fit convulsion.

Through the two-layer shroud, which was cunningly perforated to allow air in but not let germs out, Longendyke saw Barry's face changing.

This was not like the swellhead at the perimeter. Diamond-cluster crystals were forming just under the kid's skin, pricking through bloodlessly, multiplying visibly, forming a crust, roughing up against the plastic.

102

There was a crackling like the rustle of a ton of angry cellophane.

Longendyke was hit by a spasm, and pushed himself away from the kid. His hands felt filthy where he had touched the plastic, and he was shaking all over.

The Need, the needle . . .

The medics got in, and started using their own needles. 'What're you giving him?' he mumbled.

One of the medics shook a masked, hooded head. Don't ask. It was like that. He might have known.

Barry broke up inside the plastic, crystals fragmenting. Longendyke saw what was left of his face freeze, and then crack apart, falling away from what looked like a jewel-encrusted skull.

The medic held up his hypo. The needle was bent and blunted.

The crystal mass still grew and shifted. Longendyke kept his guts down by sheer force of will. What was left of Barry Bewes looked as if it ought to be sealed in a barrel and buried under a seventy-foot concrete pyramid.

Outside the faculty cottages, Jason and Abigail were kicking a football around. Abigail was out of breath, but Jason was as active as ever. She clearly relished the opportunity to break off the uneven match and talk to Brian. She knew who Monica was, and admitted when they were introduced she had not voted for her. There was an awkward pause, and Brian left the women together as he chased after Jason.

His son saw him, and took off, shouting, 'Help, there's a monster coming.'

Brian was not used to running. His lungs ached. He made a mental note to play badminton more often. Then he got his wind, and sped up. How could an eight-year-old be so fast? The kid could not read yet, but he might be shaping up as an Olympic long-distance man. Fair enough.

Jason made it halfway up the hill, towards the woods, then doubled back to hide behind one of the Halls of Residence. Brian was catching up. As he ran, he saw people at the edge of the woods. In white suits. This was a real quarantine.

'Jason, come here. This is Daddy being serious.'

'The monster! The monster!'

Brian had to stop. That was a mistake. The exertion hit him when he stood still. His knees nearly went. He filled his lungs, and started running again. Jason was weaving back towards the bulk of the campus, in the general direction of the Humanities block.

'There are no monsters,' he shouted at his son.

Students milling round stared at him. The Zombies were not too visible a presence here. Finals were on. Brian bet there would be a lot of kids around who did not even realize there was a crisis because they were so worked up over their exams.

Outside the Engineering Department, where a hallful of would-be bridge builders were bent over papers, a lone, long-haired figure in a kaftan and a bowler hat walked up and down carrying a placard. BOYCOTT FINALS. It was the least successful protest of the year, but at least it was not doing any harm.

A couple of Zombies sat by the shallow pond, which some wit had dyed fluorescent green again, eating sandwiches. So they were human after all. Another cliché bites the dust.

Jason was not flagging. The kid was not sick, although Brian thought he might be when he caught up with him.

They were past the Schools now, near the Admin blocks and the Union Building. Brian was briefly worried that Jason might trip on the paved areas and hurt himself, but the kid was too sure-footed for that. He saw his son weave his way between the casual strollers. Great. The main entrance was up ahead. The Zombies would stop Jason for him.

'Monsters, monsters, eeeeehh!'

Then Jason stopped, twenty yards short of the impromptu roadblock. Brian caught up with him, overshot by a few feet before he could stop his legs pumping pavement, and stepped back. He grabbed his son, and hugged him tight. He did not throw him in the air because, in his condition, he was not sure he could catch him.

Then the MG came out of nowhere and crashed the roadblock.

Pete felt okay. Packed all over in soft cotton wool, but okay.

They had heard the noise, and come to help him. Just a little prick in the arm, and he was okay.

They had washed the blood off, and brought him to the Infirmary.

He was not asleep. He had to answer questions. They had given him a shot to calm him down, a shot to put him to sleep, a shot to wake him up, and a shot to help him answer the questions. He had had a lot of shots.

He answered the questions, and they had let him go to bed.

He was still worried about his essay. Sometimes, he tried hard to tell the nurse that he had to go back to his room to finish it, but she did not understand.

He would have to retype the bloody pages if he were to get it in by four-thirty. He wanted to get to the dean before Bloody Basil.

They had given him a room of his own. And a pretty nurse to sit with him all the time.

He was okay.

But Something was growing in the back of his head,

Something dark and clawed and hungry and confused. That was not okay at all.

In his head, he tried to talk to the Something, to be reasonable with it. He was supposed to know about Reason. It was his field of expertise. He told the Something to be quiet, to stop playing Heavy Metal inside his brain, stopping him from doing his essay and going to sleep. It did not listen. It did not care about the Age of Reason, or his post-graduate plans, or the cotton wool.

He could not think what the Something was, but he could imagine what it was like. A little black bud, opening into a poisonous flower, blooming dark and blotting out the whiteness of the wool.

When he tried to sleep, he found he could not. He was perpetually groggy, but not tired enough to nod off. But he could dream while he was awake. He dreamed he was the Something inside himself, a confident predator certain of his First, intent on making everyone take him seriously.

He imagined taking the RG apart, pulling him limb from limb. And he felt a warm, pleasant feeling in the pit of his stomach. Then, he imagined tracking Basil down to his book-lined, fresh coffee-smelling den and dragging him out of the circle of worshipful catamites with which he had surrounded himself. He saw Basil's skin coming apart under his hands, and Basil's heart and lungs working their way out of his body.

He nodded awake, hungry, mouth dry.

Pete was okay. For now.

Cazie knew the car could take it. The man in white who got in the way bounced off the bonnet, twisted in the air, and was behind her. The wooden fence things parted in the middle, scratching the bodywork probably, and were out of the way. She left the road and drove on the lawn and the paved parts.

A man carrying a kid got out of the way. Smart move. There was something familiar about him. Brian Connors, right? The clever prick from a long time ago, yesterday.

She put the car in a pond, and vaulted out of it. A couple of guys eating their lunch looked surprised and reached out instinctively for guns they were not carrying. A few kicks took them out.

She felt great, as if she were dancing, or making love. But she had to calm down, to get herself under control.

She left the two men down and walked away. Some gaping loon asked her what was happening, and she shrugged.

'Whose car is that?'

'No idea,' she told the man in white.

'Fuck!'

'No thanks,' she smiled. 'Maybe later.'

There were enough people around, and she was fast enough for everyone to be mixed up about what they had seen.

Someone was calling her name.

'Cazie!'

There it was again, a man. She wanted a man. But she could wait. There were more important things.

'Cazie, it's me. Brian Connors, remember?'

He was panting, and holding a struggling little boy. The boy from yesterday, Jason.

'Oh hi,' she said, smiling easily, 'what's happening?'

'I don't know . . . Cazie, *what happened last night*?'

'It was cool. It's dealt with now. No worries, see.'

She held out her empty hands.

'But Rote . . .'

'Rote's out of it. It's a different game now. My game.'

'Cazie, look . . .'

She took a thumbnail between her teeth and bit. Damn, but Brian was a temptation.

107

And the boy. Jason had stopped struggling so much, and was staring at her chest, licking his teeth.

'Can't talk now. Must dash. Catch you later, right?'

His mouth fell open, in disbelief. Why was everyone so slow? Mentally, he was not yet out of the starter's gate.

She stroked the child's tender cheek, and met his gaze. She could tell he was a smart kid.

'That's a very good-looking young man you have there. Bye-bye now.'

She left him, and started walking towards York House. She needed to see Thommy and Clare.

They needed to get their show together and put it on the road.

There was a fuss outside the Hall of Residence, with lots of the men in white suits milling around. From a student she knew, Cazie learned that Clare and Thommy were in the Infirmary. The story was that one had tried to kill the other.

They had given Clare some drugs, but she had only pretended to get high. There could not be any high like the one she had had when she had turned the tables on Thommy.

Her boyfriend had been getting on her tits for months now, and this business with Rote had made it worse. Clare did not see why she should be the only one to get bruises.

She did not know why yet, but she got the feeling that suddenly she was Special.

So, when Thommy had woken her up after she had slept the morning through, she had decided to put his head through the floor.

There was nothing he could do about it.

Last night, she had been hurt. But she was better now. Better than ever.

She did not know if she had killed Thommy. She hoped so. Putting his head through the floor was the best thing she had ever done.

When the people had come for her, she had not done anything to them, although she was sure she could have shoved them into walls or folded them up and put them in briefcases. She did not see any point in spoiling the effect by overdoing it.

They brought her to the Infirmary, and gave her drugs, and strapped her down on a bed. She knew she could break the straps as if they were woven straw. They should have used something stronger.

She had told them so, but they did not pay any attention to her. That just went to show how stupid everyone else was.

Randy Preston had been just going off shift when they brought her in. She had gone out with him in the first year. Quietly, as they passed, she had bitten his hand. That was for dumping her and chasing after that slagslut Kathy Riel. He had looked meanly at her, and taken off, not even bothering with a bandage.

Now, she just looked at the white ceiling and waited for the Next Thing to happen.

There was a man in white in her room. He was not a nurse. Nurses did not have guns. And this man had a gun that looked a bit like a black T-square. She had seen them before, on TV.

It was funny. Him thinking a gun would make any difference.

Doctors had been to see her. Dr Hind, who was the campus quack, and a couple of others. They had looked at her hands, and felt her arms and legs, and asked her to open her mouth. They looked puzzled. Silly bastards.

Someone came in to check her straps. He gave new orders to the man in white, whispering. Her ears were fine-tuned. She could hear every word as if it were clearly shouted at her. She gathered that Thommy had croaked. Shame, she thought. She would have liked to hurt him some more. Nobody had said anything, but she supposed she would be in trouble about that. Police trouble. Somehow, that did not worry her too much.

The only thing that bothered Clare was her skin. It was working loose in some places. Her back felt like an itchy vest and she thought that if she broke the straps and sat up in bed it would stay on the sheet behind her. Things were bubbling inside her body.

There was a knock at the door. The man jumped, and held on to his gun.

'Who is it?'

'Visitor,' said a girl's voice. Clare recognized Cazie at once. It was like her to visit in hospital.

The man opened the door.

'How did you get in here? You're not supposed . . .'

Then Cazie punched him in the throat, sinking her fingers into him there, and lifted him up off the floor.

From the bed, Clare could see the back of the man's back, covered in white. Cazie's hand came out of it, holding something red and squelchy between her fingers. Blood leaked out like thick soup from a holed tin. Cazie dropped the thing, which hung from the hole in the man by a mess of spurting purple tubes and fatty substances. It must be his heart.

Clare saw Cazie pull her hand free, and drop the man. She had rolled up her sleeve so as not to get messy. With a towel that had been hanging by the washbasin in the room, she wiped her forearm clean, licking at the fiddly bits between her fingers to finish off the job.

'Hello, Clare, you look terrible. What happened to your face?'

'I think it's coming off.'

'That's a pity.'

'I know. I've got a funny tummy too.'

110

Cazie pulled the blankets away and looked down at her. Clare looked too. It was not pretty. Under her skin snakes were writhing. She was swelling up like the time when she thought she was pregnant.

'I can see your insides.'

'Will I die?'

'No. 'Course not. You're my friend.'

'My friend.'

Cazie bent down, below the bed, and came up again with a handful of something. She tugged, and it came free. It was the heart. She took it to the sink and washed it off.

She pinched a chunk of meat and popped it into her mouth like a grape. Cazie smiled and chewed. She sat on the edge of the bed, and took another pinch, which she put to Clare's lips.

'Here, eat this. It'll make you feel better.'

Lynch had a couple of men dead.

'. . . a blow of tremendous force. Stone's ribcage was literally pushed in. The broken bones worked like knives inside him . . .'

Matthew Gail had been medical back-up on Lynch's last few situations. He was good, dispassionate, and fast to make a diagnosis.

'A skilled fighter, then?'

Gail tugged his moustache, working his way up to saying something he thought would sound silly.

'No. The blow was way off the killpoint. It should just have dented his shoulder a bit. Nothing serious. It was the *force* that proved fatal, not the aim.'

'Shit. And Gwydion?'

'Skull. Same thing. If there weren't traces of rubber heel, I'd think it was done with a bench press.'

Lynch paused a moment, tapped his fingers against the

desk. The sheeted bodies were side by side in the back of the lorry.

'Okay, okay, screw the "softly, softly" approach.' He turned to Fassett, whose four breast-pocket pips marked him as the rank equivalent of a Sergeant-Major. 'Break out the guns, get the men armed. Put Bosworth in charge of distributing ordnance. Tell the teams to give a warning shot, if possible. If not, we'll cry tomorrow.'

He took out his own gun, and checked the clip.

Carson had put all the specs on 125 through the computer, and given Anderton the read-out.

It was bad news.

Anderton felt sick. He looked again, and the same conclusions came to him.

Carson stood at his elbow, waiting for a verbal report. Finch was still fiddling about with 126 dishes. Tripps, Lynch's man, was looking bored, but standing alert.

They could still walk about, but Anderton knew they were dead people.

Like him.

He had been chain-popping aspirins all day, but the headache had not gone away. The churning in his stomach got worse every half hour or so, in perceptible lurches. Anderton had seen Finch take off her glasses and rub her temples too many times. Carson's acne was starting to dribble.

'We've got it,' he said quietly.

'Yes?'

'125. It doesn't die with the host. It's communicable. Highly communicable.'

Carson hit him in the stomach, savagely. Anderton doubled over and was sick. Tripps levelled his gun.

Carson, his trousers stained with Anderton's bile, whirled like a dervish, sweeping a benchtop clear of

112

retorts and dishes. Glass broke. A patch of skin dislodged from Carson's cheek and splattered on the tile floor. Bone shone yellow in the raw hole. He had a triangular wedge of broken glass in his hand.

The glass slashed in front of Anderton's face. The scientist flinched, and banged his head against the bench. Carson raised the glass again, and a neat row of holes opened in his chest. Anderton did not hear the noise of Tripps's gun until seconds later, when Carson was already pitched forward on top of him.

He felt teeth go in somewhere below his collarbone. The body was pulled roughly off him, and he stood up.

Tripps had put his faceplate on, and looked like something from outer space. Anderton held up red hands.

'It's in the blood,' he said.

Inside his mask, Tripps's face burst. His perspex eyeholes went red, as if his entire head had turned liquid. He stayed standing for a long moment, then crumpled like an empty suit. The seals were good, there was no leakage, but he did not keep his manshape. The chest fell in, and the limbs ballooned.

Anderton had a nasty desire to step on the suit, to see if it would squelch open like a slug.

He was bleeding himself, from somewhere. He had had 125 for over a day now. Probably caught it from Skippy's remains. The incubation period must be erratic. Tripps could not have been exposed for more than half an hour.

Even without the break-in, he would have caught 125 and Lynch would be here with Unwin's gladiators.

'Fuck UCC! Fuck everything!'

Finch helped him up.

'Fuck me,' she whispered.

Her blouse was open, and her third teeth were coming through. She kissed him. He could not feel anything. She permanently put his lips out of shape. Strange flesh.

Anderton pushed Finch away, and looked at his hands.

113

The skin was mostly gone. He saw muscles sliding off bone. He would not have the use of them much longer.

And he had something to do.

Pain shot up from his fingers as he prised Tripps's gun free.

He shot Finch once, in the heart. He had always liked her.

'Fuck me . . . me . . . me . . .'

She ran down like a talking doll as her brain died on her.

Anderton found that his forefinger had come off in the trigger guard. It was stuck. He felt as if his hands were being eaten by army ants. He could not use the right at all.

He poked the finger out of the guard with a pencil, and rested the gun butt on the floor. He put the barrel to the bridge of his nose, and worked the trigger with his left thumb.

The gun was emptying itself into the ceiling a full minute later.

From the kitchen of Brian's house, they heard the first shots. He flashbacked to Grosvenor Square, 1971, and the spurt of flame in the dark, Jean's knee a shattered ruin, the goggle-eyed face of the teen marine with the shaking gun, the sudden rush of sobriety.

'What the fuck?' shouted Monica. Jason giggled at the bad word. Brian listened, and heard the typewriter noise again.

'That's not a rabbit hunt.'

Abigail had dropped her cup of tea. The mug had not shattered, but the floor was soaked.

They could not see anything, so they had to go outside.

'Abigail,' Brian said, 'keep Jason here. Lock up. You

114

can stay the night. If anyone but us comes to the door, pretend you're not in. And keep him quiet if you have to gag him.'

The girl was trembling, an Alice overcome by Wonderland. He hoped she would be able to hang together.

'You understand?'

'Y – yes . . .'

Jason pulled at Abigail's arm. 'Can we watch a video, Abi, can we?'

Brian nodded, and the girl took his son into the living room. Jason was frisky, but unhurt. Thank God. It all seemed like a game. Monica had her coat on, and the door open.

He did not want to leave Jason, but there was no choice. He knew his son was safe; now, he should try to help Monica, to do what best he could for everyone . . .

Outside, the campus looked normal at first. There was no more shooting. As they walked towards the main buildings, they saw a lot of people milling about. There were a few Zombies around, but mostly it was just University people. A guy Brian knew from the School of European Studies asked him if he knew what was going on, and he had to shrug a 'no' at him. A girl was having hysterics by the Refectory, and three of her friends were calming her down.

Apart from the men in white, it could have been any late afternoon.

'Where's Lynch?' Monica spat.

'God knows. Where did the shooting come from?'

'Shooting!' said a bystanding student, taking it up and passing it on. 'Shooting! Someone's been shot!'

Brian knew this was how panics got started.

'East Slope, I think. The Infirmary?'

The men in white started running at the same time, as if worked by magic. They must have intercoms in their suits. They were headed for the East Slope. And they had guns out.

'I said no guns,' Monica said.

Someone got in the way, and was knocked down.

'Fascist bastards.'

The Zombie stopped, twenty yards beyond the fallen boy, and turned to look at the group of two or three angry students gathered around him. He had a pistol out, and his mask on.

'Fascist *bastard*!'

A book flew through the air towards him, whirling like a discus. It glanced off his raised arm. The Zombie fired once, into the air above him. The group froze like a tableau.

'Heav-*vee*!'

The Zombie pointed his gun at the kids for an instant, then turned and resumed running.

There was more shooting from the East Slope, impossibly loud now they were out in the open. As a man, the group of students hurled themselves flat on the ground like refugees from a '50s civil defence drill, arms over their heads.

Monica was off and running, after the Zombies. Brian knew better, but had to go with her.

A klaxon sounded, and a loudspeaker voice started to read a bland reassurance he did not have the time or the inclination to listen to.

The place was becoming a battlefield.

Shaun Bensom did not believe in Finals. He had worked hard for three years, turning in essays, projects, original work. He had had practical experience in the summer vacs, on building sites and in a draughtsman's office. He had proved everything he wanted to, and he knew his marks in continuous assessment were way above average.

But why should his degree depend on the state of his stomach and his head on a single, solitary afternoon in May? What if he had 'flu? Or some personal crisis? And what if the paper – like last year's – was entirely concerned with some obscure facet of claw-feed grinding he had no intention of ever getting involved with in his professional life? He had earned the title Engineer, and two hours bending his back over a desk would not make any difference. It would just be jumping through another hoop.

He had been walking up and down outside the exam hall since the others had gone in, crossing his picket line of one. His placard felt a lot heavier than it had done at first.

There were a lot of people running about the campus today, making a noise. If he had been inside, he would have found it bloody hard to concentrate despite the thick windows. Some street theatre group were playing spacemen all over the place, and waving toy guns. It must be like that Assassination game, where middle management stalked each other through the woods and shot their opponents with paint pellets.

No one was paying any attention to his protest, although he had heard some sniggering from the other students before the exam started. Hetty had said she would bring him a coffee and some salad rolls from the canteen when her tutorial was over, but she had not shown up. He was hungry. At least it was summer, and not quite freezing.

Over by the Humanities Block, the Game was getting out of hand. He saw a guy in leathers jump on one of the spacemen, and get his head kicked in. It was some sort of martial arts display. Shaun bet it hurt. The spaceman shot the leathers guy in the head, and even from two hundred yards, he could see there was an extremely large gobbet of red paint.

Silly buggers!

He wished he was back in his flat, passing joints with Hetty and Colin and Liz Donoghue. But he had his stand to make, his principles to uphold.

No one was looking. He rested his placard against a low wall, its message out so people could see, and lit up a fag. Under the cold sun, he felt sleepy.

The students inside would be on the home stretch now. All but the real dumbos would be through with the stress question and onto the plane drawing. Pencil-pushing geeks! Colin was in there somewhere. Sold out by his best mate, Shaun thought, what a world! Finals bring out the worst.

The spacemen were dragging off the leathers guy. He must be out cold. These martial arts people could get out of hand too easily.

He turned and looked at the hall. Through the plate-glass windows, he could see the rows and rows of desks, and the ranks of bowed heads. One or two smug bastards had finished already, and were sitting back, taking it easy. The real clever-clevers had finished, but were going through their papers making minor adjustments.

Colin was near the front, still writing. They had had an argument about all this last night and it had come down to Colin agreeing with everything Shaun said but still swearing he would sit his Finals.

'After all, I want the bloody degree . . .'

Colin would be moving out of the flat soon if Shaun could help it. It meant losing Liz Donoghue and her dope connection, but principles were principles and he would stand by his.

Colin was slowing down. He put his pencil down, and rubbed his nose. Shaun saw it was bleeding.

That's exactly what he meant! A chance nosebleed at this of all times, brought on by stress probably, and you knew no assessor in the world was going to give higher

118

than a Third to a paper with blood all over it. It was so blatantly unfair!

Colin would agree with him now.

Blood was streaming out of both his nostrils, and he was smearing it over his face like a spreading moustache. He must not have a handkerchief. Colin stood up, and fell over. The desk next to his went down under him, and Gilly Walker – one of the few girls in the School – had to jump out of his way.

Colin must be having an acid flashback. He had spent his first year at University swallowing tabs like they were polo mints.

Watching his flatmate writhe around on the floor, while chaos rippled out from him, was sort of funny, but a bit depressing. The glass was well soundproofed, so Shaun could not hear if there was an uproar or not. The invigilator was walking towards the incident.

Shaun turned his back on it all, and picked up his placard.

'What is this?'

Monica shouted at the Zombies. They were crouched in ones and twos around the Infirmary Building, taking cover behind signs and steps. A few turned their heads, but generally she was ignored.

A window in the building was broken from the inside. Curtains waved and there was gunfire. A line of divots popped up in the tarmac of the car park, and the ambulance's left rear tyre burst.

Monica felt herself going down, and for an insane moment thought she had been shot. But it was Brian, pulling her behind a rubbish skip.

'What is this?' she said again, to no one in particular.

The black Zombie with the walkie-talkie must be Lynch. He was buzzing orders into it.

119

There was quiet for a few seconds, then two Zombies stood up and sprayed the front of the Infirmary with machine-gun fire. Infinity loops of bullet pocks appeared in the walls of the prefab building. Brown hardwood flowers bloomed in the white-painted facade.

Answering fire came from inside the building, but it was random, directionless. A nearby shrub was whipped with bullets.

'There's someone crazy in there,' Brian said.

'Let's get closer, talk to Lynch,' she insisted.

'No. He's busy.'

More orders crackled. Monica could not make them out. Then Lynch was up himself, firing from the hip. His gun was bigger and louder than any she had seen so far. The Infirmary door, decorated in bright colours at the Kids' Karnival last week, fell apart, and came off its hinges in pieces.

The Zombies dashed forwards. The first to the door bounced back, as if off an invisible wall, and Monica saw blood streaming from his chest.

Brian tried to push her head down so she would not see any more, but she fought him.

The Zombie was dead in the doorway, and something was moving inside the building. There were men either side of the door, backs to the wall, guns pointed upwards. One nodded to the other, and swung into the gap, firing wild. His gun must have jammed, because the noise shut off suddenly as he vanished inside. Monica thought he had been pulled into the darkness by something.

After a beat, the crazy people came out. Some had guns, most did not. They wore hospital gowns, pyjamas, doctors' coats, even Zombie whites. And their faces were not real. Some were bleeding.

In the lead, clutching the captured Zombie by his crooked neck, was Cazie Bruckner.

Only she did not look like Cazie any more.

Lynch pulled down his mask and shouted, 'Shoot the bastards, now!'

The man Cazie was holding got shot. She could feel the bullets punching into him. He was big, and she could hide behind him. Dead, he weighed more, but struggled less.

The rest of the world was in slow motion. She could see the bullets in the air, whirling as they came. The men in the white hoods had not a hope.

She knew a couple of the less important ones had been killed in the break-out. The new-made ones. She hoped Clare had come through. The others did not matter.

She had the dead man's gun jammed through his armpit. Taking his weight on one hand, she got hold of the stock and started firing at the men in white suits.

The white stood out very nicely against the redbrick walls and green grass. Shooting them was too easy.

She slung the dead man away, hurling him one-handed. He came down twenty feet or more away in a jumble of awkwardly bent arms and legs.

The gun was all used up, so she threw it away.

The others had fanned out either side of her. Several of them were down, but most were off and running.

It would spread. They could not stop her.

She ran straight ahead, leaning out of the way of the bullets, swiping the white hoods aside. Each time she connected, she heard bones breaking, and the slow trickle of an internal injury.

Jesus, these were the days to be alive!

She vaulted a wall, and put on a burst of speed.

Lynch fired at the crazy bitch as she disappeared like a cat over the wall. Brick chips flew, but she was gone.

He took a damage reading. Three, no, four men down.

The enemy – whatever the hell they were – had suffered more. There were seven dead things on the Infirmary forecourt.

Two of them were once his own men. Even with their masks off, he could not recognize them. He would pull tags later.

'What is going on? What the fuck is going on?'

It was Flint, the student *Presidente*, with the nonentity from Jackson's office. Damn civilians!

'Epidemic.'

His men were regrouping. He would need more people to handle this.

'Of what, Lynch?'

'I told you, I'm not a scientist. They call it Batch 125, if that means anything.'

'It makes people crazy, right?'

Lynch was not giving anything away.

'What's it *for*, Lynch?'

He looked at her, and saw fear inside her tough eyes.

'Guess,' he said.

Jason still had not calmed down. Abigail had had to go through ten or a dozen video tapes. He would sit for anything between three seconds and two minutes on fast-forward before deciding he wanted something different.

If she thought about it, she would be grateful for the distraction. She did not want to have to face up to whatever else was going on. Brian and Monica Flint had not been expansive, but whatever it was was very scary.

'Hate this! Gimme 'nother!'

'What do we say, Jason? Please?'

'Gimme *'nother*!'

He was pushing his jaw out, trying to look fierce.

'Jason.'

'Gimme!'

122

He grabbed at her with both hands, sinking his little fingers into her middle. It hurt. She would have bruises.

'Gimme!'

'Jason, no. We don't talk to people like that.'

The boy head-butted her in the stomach, winding her. Christ, he was turning into a little monster!

'Jason, no. That's too rough.'

He let her go, and glared up at her. Abigail remembered how powerless she had always felt in the presence of adults. In Jason's eyes, she could see dull resentment, but also something else . . . An animal cunning she had never come across in a kid before. She did not like it.

'Let's make you some tea, shall we? There's cake and biscuits.'

Jason threw back his head and howled like a wolf, 'Hun-*greee*!'

There was something wrong with his teeth, something wrong with his mouth. It should not be able to open that wide. He would do himself an injury.

Abigail held his chin, and closed his mouth.

'If you go around like that, Jason, a bird will come and nest in it.'

She turned her back on him and went into the kitchen. That was her mistake.

He must have sprung like a coyote. She felt the impact on her upper back, forcing her forward. His hands were in her hair, pulling.

'Ow, Jason. Cut it out. Come on.'

She wriggled, trying to dislodge him, but he was holding fast. His knees gripped her sides, and one arm was around her neck. She could not talk. Her hair was in her mouth.

She did not want to hurt him, but she might have to.

His hand passed in front of her face, and she felt an icy touch near her ear. Something wet.

He had cut her.

123

She tottered into the living room, and hurled him free. He shot into the sofa, and bounced up and down laughing.

She put her hand to her temple. It came away bloody.

'Jason, your nails are too long.'

Suddenly, he was still, tense as an armed mantrap. And as dangerous. Abigail started thinking seriously about protecting herself. His eyes looked yellowish now, with tiny pupils. He looked hungry.

There were knives in the kitchen.

She could not believe she had thought about that. This was an eight-year-old boy, not Jack the Ripper.

Just now, there was something very adult, unhealthily adult, about the way Jason was looking at her.

'Abi . . . hun-*greeeeee*!'

He licked his lips. No tongue could be that long. He shrugged, and ripped his shirt. He pulled at his collar. Buttons popped, and cloth tore.

Abigail could not take her eyes off him.

Just inside the kitchen, on a side-table, there was a half-full bottle of Perrier water. She thought she could pick it up and use it faster than he could strike, but she was not sure.

She did not want to bet her life on it.

She put out a hand behind her, and found the door-jamb, held it.

Jason just looked.

He was squirming now, with barely repressed energy. He was a growing boy. She could *see* him growing.

'Jason,' she whispered, pleading, 'Jason, don't . . .'

Then he came at her.

Pete had been shot in the side, but did not notice much. When he was away from the Infirmary, he hiked up his bloody pyjama jacket and saw the hole. It was puckered up, but healing over nicely.

By the campus clock, it was four-fifteen. He still had a quarter of an hour. Realistically, he knew he could not get his essay typed up and ready in time. But he could show up in person and plead his case.

He thought he could convince the dean.

There were people running all around, and firing off guns. But he ignored them.

The steps to the School of English and American Studies were up ahead. His bare feet were frozen by the concrete slabs, but he hopped up them and pushed through the main doors under the Humanities H structure, getting good rubber under his soles.

Inside, things were much quieter. There was a Godard film showing in A2, and a steady dribble of students were walking out on it, yawning and complaining.

He was having to get used to his strength. Opening the door to the stairwell, he wrenched it off its hinges and had, embarrassedly, to lean it up against a wall, hoping no one would notice. His muscles were expanded inside his striped pyjamas, straining the seams.

Up on the Eng/Am floor, outside the dean's office, there was a minimal queue of his coursemates, waiting to hand over their take-away papers. Bloody Basil, pouting smugly, was glancing over his catamites' papers, making jokes and dishing out complacent reassurances. His own essays were in an imitation leather folder, done up with a bow of red ribbon. Bloody Basil had a word processor with a presentation-standard printer, and all his essays looked like published articles.

'Petah, my dear colleague,' Basil said, seeing him for the first time, 'how perfectly shocking you look. If there is any weather about, you certainly seem to have stumbled under it.'

One of Basil's gunsels giggled, handing over his own essay to the dean's secretary.

Pete loped up to Basil, feeling the strength in his insteps and thighs as he walked.

'Care to take a glance?' Basil said, offering his essay for inspection. 'A modest effort, but one hopes it will suffice.'

Pete took the essay, and opened the folder. Basil had chosen to answer the Porson question. '"When Dido found Aeneas would not come,"' he read, '"she mourned in silence and was Di-do-dum," Richard Porson, *Epigram on Latin Gerunds*.'

Only Basil would even have attempted the fucking Porson question!

He looked at Basil's foot-wide smile.

'Porson, eh?'

Basil nodded, barely able to contain his glee within his checked trousers.

'1759 – 1808?'

Basil swelled with undisguised pride.

'"I went to Frankfort, and got drunk,

"With that most learn'd professor, Brunck,"' Pete quoted.

'Ah-hah,' Basil countered, '"I went to Wortz, and got more drunken,

"With that more learn'd professor, Ruhnken."'

The catamites all but clapped their leader's erudition.

Some time after Porson's death, his executors had been sorting through the books and papers in his library and kept coming across green hairy things stuck between pages. The scholar and wit had been in the habit of using unwanted sandwiches as bookmarks.

Pete rolled up Basil's essay like a scroll, enjoying the sparks of dismay in his eyes. He put his forefinger and thumb into the lizard's mouth, keeping it open like a letterbox, and posted the essay into his oesophagus. With the heel of his hand, he rammed the folder in past Basil's tonsils, scraping chunks out of his throat.

The catamites were aghast, and the secretary fainted. Basil was on the floor now, foaming and choking around his learned critique of the childish humour of the author of *Facetiae Cantabrigienses*. Yellow and white foam came out of Basil's mouth, soaking around the essay and dribbling down onto the pleated collar of his affected smoking jacket. The scholar twitched and spasmed on the carpet, squawking in a most un-Johnsonian display of undignified pain.

Pete needed a piss, and Basil's face was there handy as a target. He took his dick out of his pyjamas, aimed it, and let go.

Abigail woke up, and could not believe what Jason was doing to her.

His face was above hers, and she felt his tongue on her eyelids, lips, cheeks, nose. He was panting hard, and strings of spittle fell from his mouth. Cords in his neck were working ferociously. Behind his little boy face, was a calculated adult cruelty, a wish for power over others, a need for brutal dominance.

He was still child-sized, and his body did not match hers. Small as she was, he was smaller. If his face was pressed to her neck, his knees were at her hips, his feet trailing between her thighs.

Her clothes were mostly torn away, and his hands were on her. Her flat breasts hurt where his fingers had clawed. He had chewed her neck, but not broken the skin. Blue bruises circled her throat like a necklace. She thought he might have stove in a couple of her ribs.

She could not feel anything below the waist, which was probably just as well. She thought he had not been able to get into her, and was thrusting his hips against her soft stomach.

127

He obviously wanted to rape her, but did not quite know how.

Surprisingly, she could dissociate herself from this. It was as if she were a ghost standing in the doorway, looking down on the child-thing and her former body. There must be streaks of red on her white skin. Her hair was a tangle over her face. She felt a broken tooth in her mouth, and one of her eyes was swelling shut.

When Jason was finished, if he *could* finish, he would kill her. But she really did not have a lot to say about that any more.

The numbness was creeping up.

Monica was resisting him, but he pulled her by the hand.

Most people were dashing about at random. But Brian knew where he was going.

'The Admin Building. We've got to see Jackson.'

Lynch could not be allowed to deal with this on his own. His idea of therapy was a bullet in the brain. They needed paramedics, not mercenaries.

Brian thought he was the only one thinking clearly on campus.

'Useless . . . useless . . .'

She stopped fighting him, and let herself be led. That was one worry less, he thought.

The gunfire was constant now, from all over the campus. By the canteen, they saw a crowd of things – infectees? – corner a Zombie and take him apart. He emptied his gun into them, but they did not take any notice until it was all over. Then they died, mostly.

Some of them he still recognized.

On a grassy slope, one of the cleaners was battering a Professor of Anthropology with a broom. Brian could not tell which was the sick one.

The Admin Building forecourt was deserted. There were not even any bodies.

Should they get in one of the cars and high-tail it the hell out of there? No, there was Jason. Anyway, he did not know how to hotwire a car. He half-thought that was just one of those things you only saw in films and television shows.

The uniformed porter was still on duty in the reception area. He waved to Brian and Monica as they passed. Probably, fifty per cent of the people on campus still did not think there was anything wrong.

How could they ignore all this fucking bang-bang?

They went up the stairs. The place was just as it always was. Posters advertising plays and concerts were neatly pinned to the walls. The large windows let in late afternoon sunlight. It was warm and airy.

Upstairs, someone was typing.

There had not been a P.A. announcement for a while. Jackson was letting things lie.

'Monica, this way.'

He hoped she was not going catatonic on him.

The V-C's suite was still open.

Inside, there was a mess.

Jackson sat on the imitation leather settee in his reception room, long, dark, stains on his suit, his face white as wax. In his lap, he had Gabrielle's head. He was stroking her hair, crooning something to himself.

The rest of Gabrielle was still at her desk.

'Hello, Brian. It's been a bad day for us all, hasn't it?'

Jackson lurched forwards, as if about to be sick, and coughed up a long, ragged snake. It dangled from his mouth like a particularly vile old school tie.

The Vice-Chancellor's head hung uselessly, but the snake – new organ, whatever? – darted about, alert. There was an eye where its head should have been, blinking sideways.

Things began to push at Jackson's suit from the inside. Damp patches appeared.

Gabrielle's head fell from his lap and rolled across the floor.

What had been Jackson stood up. His old flesh hung like a tramp's suit on the living skeleton of new growth. Feeble hands were pushing his clothes apart. The cobra-necked eye looked at Brian, then at Monica.

He could not read any expression in the thing.

Brian picked up a tubular steel hatstand and held it like a lance. The Jackson-Thing staggered forward. One foot came off, and it steadied itself with a three-fingered hand that squeezed out of the raw ankle.

Brian realized that Monica had been screaming since they had come into the room.

Conquering his disgust, he rammed Jackson with the hatstand. The circular base sunk slightly into his chest, and flesh lapped around it. The thing was forced back against a bookcase, trapped. The snake growth stretched towards him.

He pushed hard on the hatstand, mashing the thing. There was blood, and a thick, yellow liquid that fell in splashes on the carpet.

He pulled the stand back, letting Jackson fall, then started using it as a long bludgeon, pounding again and again into the unrecognizable mass of swelling, bleeding, contracting, formless flesh.

After a long time, it stopped being anything except a stain.

With a roar, Brian threw the ruined hatstand through the picture window. It hung in the air for a moment in a cloud of glass shards that caught and reflected the sunlight, and then fell out of sight.

Cool air rushed in. And the sound of gunfire.

Monica had stopped screaming. Brian was drained, had nothing left to feel. He turned to her, and she threw herself into his arms. He hugged her tight, needing her as much as she needed him.

Over her shoulder, he saw Gabrielle stand up, purple feelers extended from her neck like a ruff.

If anything had happened, it was over. Jason had left her alone.

She could feel herself again. There was a stickiness on her stomach, but not between her legs. However he had changed, he still could not manage that much.

Abigail thought she would die a virgin.

She tried to get up, but nothing seemed to work. There was pain behind her eyes, and under her scalp.

Jason was still in the house, still dangerous. She should make an effort. He was only eight; he had proved that he could not rape her, and she was damned if he was going to kill her.

She was unsteady on her legs, and felt silly in her scraps of clothing. There was nothing in the room for her to wear.

Looking down at her too-thin, too-young body, she saw the cuts. She had not bled much at all, as if the marks were just red biro lines on her skin. But she tingled all over.

She walked into the kitchen, and put on a cooking apron. It had a big, primary-coloured apple on it. She still had her shoes, and most of her skirt. She felt decent.

Then she took a knife, choosing the straight-edged carving implement over the serrated breadknife. She did not hold it overarm like a silly girl in a horror film, but like a switchblade, so she could slash and stab.

God knows where you learn all this stuff. Television, probably.

'Jason,' she shouted, 'you can come out now. Abi's not angry.'

Silence.

'We'll have some cake.'

A growling, somewhere upstairs.

She was not stupid. He would have to come for her.

She hunkered down in the hall, facing the stairs, and waited.

He was only a boy; he was not patient at all. Inside two minutes, the study door opened, and he came out.

He had grown, but he was still a boy. His legs were hairy, but white patches showed through at the knees. His genitalia were ridiculously, cherubically small. He had pulled on a T-shirt with a picture of Batman on it.

'Abi . . . still hun-*greee*!'

'Come down and eat, you chickenshit cocksucking little bastard you!'

She had never used words like that before. He giggled. Little boys like to be shocked.

'Motherfucker!'

He came down the stairs, laughing and snarling. He was still slobbering.

She held the knife tightly. Its sharp edge glinted in the last of the daylight in the hall.

She imagined traced lines on his body, where she would cut.

'Cunt-eater!'

Three steps from the bottom, he tensed to leap. She extended the knife before her.

Jason pushed himself into the air, and hit her. The knife went into him somewhere. They were thrown back against the front door. The Chubb lock burst.

Stumbling backwards on the porch, Abigail kicked a pair of milkbottles aside. She fell, and Jason was on top of her, clawing and scratching.

She stabbed upwards, sawing into his flesh, grinding against his ribs, pulling free, and stabbed again.

She stood up, and Jason fell off her. He tried to crawl

away, towards the fence that bounded the cottage's postage-stamp garden. He tore at the earth, uprooting herbs and vegetables.

Abigail bent over him, and stabbed him in the back. She slashed across the back of his neck, opening him to the bone.

When it was done, she kicked him to make sure, and sat down by the fence, waiting to be rescued.

It was all over.

She still held the knife, just in case, but she did not need it. Jason was done with, over with.

A man with a mask on came, and she knew he would rescue her. She stood up to throw her arms around his neck, to kiss his mask, to sob on his shoulder, to thank him . . .

. . . but he shot her.

'Christ, what a mess!'

Anderton had not gone out easily. Lynch saw that the scientist had redecorated the ceiling with his brains. Droplets were still forming and falling in the laboratory.

It was all falling apart.

'Where's Gail?' he asked Fassett. 'I need some expert opinion.'

'We had to shoot him, Frank. He freaked.'

'Shit. What about the University doc, Hind?'

'He went down with the others at the Infirmary.'

Lynch was tired. He knew they were probably all dead by now. He had had his mask off too often. They all had.

'And Bosworth isn't responding either.'

Lynch thought it through, and did not get a pleasing result.

'Sir,' buzzed in his ear, 'call for you in the mobile H.Q.'

He tapped his mike. 'Patch it through.'

A voice he recognized but could not put a name to

came on. 'Lynch, we've been following the print-outs. You've got a fuck-up situation.'

'You're telling me. When are your experts coming?'

'Never. We've redrawn the scenario. We've got to contain this. I'm sending you a suitcase. We'll have you out of there, and a cover ready.'

He did not argue. It was probably worth losing half the country to get this bug the hell off the face of the Earth.

'When?'

'The chopper's on the way. Deal with this in a soonest-possible mode.'

The voice was gone. The thing in his ear was dead.

Shit, shit, shit.

No way would UCC bring him out, or any of his team. They were just potential infection vectors like the rest.

But he did not feel any different in himself.

Something Anderton had tried to say earlier came back to him. 125 was not necessarily a disease. What had he called it, a symbiote? Perhaps this would not be too bad after all. And the suitcase might be useful.

'Fassett, let's take this place off the map.'

'Frank?'

'We've got the phones, right? Put them out of commission forever. Have the men shoot anyone trying to leave, crazy or not. Let's retake this fucking place and establish ourselves some sort of control, okay?'

'Yes, Frank.'

He could not believe it!

Willard Longendyke thought of himself as a scumbag, but this chick had hacked up some kid with a fucking carving knife.

He had shot chicks before. In the Zone, and with the teams. One of the towelhead 'ters' had been a German broad. Ugly fuck with a face like a horse's rear end.

134

This girl looked about fourteen. The sort to wait for Lassie to come home and to be friends with Flicka.

He was shaking in his suit.

The Need, the Need, the Need . . .

Someone shouted at him, and he whirled, firing from the hip. Old dude in a leather jacket, standing by a motorsickle. His chest blew up.

The Bozz Man was in sight. He came over, assessed the situation, and nodded approval.

Longendyke had to get away.

He had a bellyful of snakes, and every square inch of his skin was on the move. Sweat bunched his suit at the ankles, crotch and armpits.

The Bozz Man jogged off.

Fuck this shit!

He scragged the Sergeant-Equivalent neatly, one shot to the back of the head, pushing him away, shoving him down.

He did not feel any different.

He had been gulping back vomit all day. Now, he was on the verge of getting under control.

One jab, and he would fly.

No one had seen him bring down the Bozz Man.

That was chilly, then.

He left the dead girl where she was, and ran past the cooling Sergeant-Equivalent, looking for the building he had been in earlier. Most of that was roped off-limits. He could find a quiet, undisturbed corner there and treat himself to the needle.

Everything was about to come together, to make sense.

Gabrielle was easier to deal with than Jackson had been. Brian just knocked her down with a bodyblow, and she was like a turtle on its back. Without a head, you do not have much of a sense of balance.

135

Monica snatched up Gabrielle's telephone. She held the receiver out to him. Nothing.

'Lynch is closing us down.'

'Bastard.'

Now what? Brian had no ideas. He could not do anything to save the world any more. There was only his own.

'Jason. We've got to get Jason. And get out.'

That meant a trip across campus. Less than half a mile. But half a mile through a combat zone.

'My car,' said Monica. 'It's by the Union Building, across the square.'

'You're an angel.'

'Not yet.'

'Let's go.'

Pete thought he would drop by the York House bar and have a drink.

There were people running all over the place, but so long as he walked nobody took much notice of him. He had on a duffel coat he had found lying abandoned, and there was some money in it. That was good luck.

The bar was packed, as usual. It had just opened. He saw Neil, Phil and Stef in their usual corner, with a tableful of pint glasses in front of them. There was loud music playing.

His mates were sitting with Harry the Hack, the University's writer-in-residence. A master of post-modern horror, Harry was supposed to be teaching a course on James Herbert, but had not bothered to turn up for any of his scheduled lectures. Apparently, he had spent almost all his time on campus drinking and being ill.

'. . . What you have to understand about *Land of the Giants*,' Harry was saying, 'is that it demonstrates Irwin

Allen's recurring theme that man's ambitions should exceed his grasp. Hey, Pete . . .'

They all turned to look at him. They were surprised to see him. The bar went quiet like in a Western when Gary Cooper walks in.

Pete was about to order a round, when he realized how unfair it was. He always had to be first to dig into his pocket. The others always hung back. Phil only bought rounds when there was just the two of them, and Neil kept going on about the cashpoint not working and being out of readies. They could buy their own from now on.

'You should be in the hospital, guy,' said Stef. 'You look like shit.'

'I'm fine,' he said, 'just fine.'

A pinball machine was clanging and clattering in the recreation room next to the bar. He could hear it, and a lot of other things. Radios, conversations, shuffling feet, clanking glasses, running water.

A tall student in a football shirt pushed past him, on the way to the bar. He did not say 'excuse me' or anything, so Pete took his windpipe out of his neck, cut it in half with his teeth, and let it dangle.

There was a lot more noise. He could not identify it.

Air was whistling through the tube he had yanked out of the rude student's throat. And blood spurted like water from a ruptured hose.

Pete put his mouth to the geyser, and had his drink. The bar was empty by the time he had finished, and all the tables were turned over. Neil, Phil and Stef had left their pints unfinished, but he did not fancy the piss-poor beer you got here. Only Harry the Hack stayed, and he was trying to focus on his whisky, mumbling about Lacanian tropes in *The Magic Cottage*.

Pete went to the rec room, to see if he could scare up a game of pool.

There was nobody playing there. Nobody there at all,

in fact, except for the man in the white suit with the gun. He did not look like a pool player.

The man's aim was low. Pete saw holes going into his stomach, but could not feel anything. He was sure his gut could chew the lead slugs up. It had before. There were ropes of flesh growing under his jacket, like potato tubers. He did not know what they were, but his body seemed to have it under control.

The man shot him again, in the head this time.

He felt the metal in his brain, felt his cerebral tissue clustering around it, making walnut-size pearls of thinking matter.

One by one, his senses went out, leaving him in the dark.

He could not move any more, but he could think.

He thought he was still growing.

Cazie was Queen of the Hill.

She had people with her now, people who were beginning to understand. Clare was a help, of course. Always Clare, always there. She was on the roof of the School of English and American Studies, with the first of her followers.

'Go with it,' Cazie told a kid just wriggling through his clothes. 'Let your body find its new form. It'll be right for you, I promise.'

The others stood in a circle as she coaxed the true thing out of the old shell. Hair fell off like a wig, and his head swelled like a soft-shelled egg. He was going to be bright.

'Beautiful,' purred Clare, taking the new man's hand.

Clare was not raw any more. She had strikingly beautiful scales that reflected the sunset like prisms.

They had guns, of course. Picked up from the men in white, donated by those outsiders who had accepted the new ways. But they would not need guns much longer.

There were other ways of getting what they wanted. Special ways. Cazie was still learning, but a whole universe was opening up before her. She could taste everything, feel everything, be everything.

Unlike many of the others, she still looked much as she had once done. Although when she held her hand up, she could see the bones glowing inside, stronger, more complicated than they had been before. She felt her brain changing, multiplying its strength inside her skull. That was her way of changing, she knew. She was moving into the dark areas of the brain that most people never use.

The change was a fulfilment of human potential.

Some of the others were discovering their new channels of pleasure. Groups of two or three or four clung together, penetrating, loving, giving. It was a good way to start. Eventually, there would be children. A pure new generation. Babies who had never been human.

With every minute, she had more at her side, more converts, more disciples.

The boy prone on the concrete stiffened, and metallic arches erupted from him, gathering into a crustacean-like construction. It skittered away from what it had been.

Cazie turned her head up to the skies, and ululated. A long, low note began in her stomach and rang out over the campus, calling to the newborns, warning those who would cling to the past.

The sun was going down on the old humanity.

PART THREE

Graduation

On a fluorescent panel inset into the ceiling of the main laboratory, the virus designated Batch 125, present in highly concentrated form in the brain tissue formerly lodged in the skull of Dr Xavier Anderton, began to think by itself.

What little was left of Dr Anderton was surprised. 125 had been interesting, but this was unprecedented. As the viral thoughts expanded, forming a rudimentary consciousness, Anderton's lingering mind faded slowly to black.

Warmed by the heat and light behind the plastic panel, Batch 125 progressed rapidly from sentience to sapience, compounding its vague first impressions with scraps of Anderton's memory. It had an idea of what it was, and of its special powers and capabilities.

It could grow, and so it did.

Greyish tissue ballooned and spread, dendrons forming, synapses sparking. Its consciousness moved into the empty brain cells, expanding literally and figuratively. Already, it was moving, and thinking, in three dimensions. Nerve tangles sprouted, and dangled like tendrils, feeling around in an increasingly methodical manner.

There were four dead people in the room, saturated with 125. Each of them could be useful to the newborn.

The nerves thickened, coated themselves with fibrelike skin, and became tipped with bony barbs. These sank into the remains of Donald Carson, Elizabeth Finch, Xavier Anderton and Kevin Tripps. Viral clusters came together, and barely animated corpses began to move experimentally. 125 played with its extended body/bodies, increasing its control over its movements.

143

It experienced pleasure.

Finch, the least damaged, was the first of its components to get up on its feet. The others soon joined it, joined with it. 125 pulled itself together, and sloughed off the irredeemably dead flesh. The still-growing, still-changing portions formed the beginnings of a serviceable body. Finch, Carson and Tripps contributed new cranial matter, and this was suctioned up through a new-formed tube, globbing around the thinking remains of Dr Anderton, forming a fully-functional, surprisingly well-balanced thinking centre for the virus. Finch and Carson were the core of its musculature, but Tripps, whose flesh was virtually liquefied, provided easily accessible bones for moulding and redistribution.

Whatever it touched, it could change.

Through Finch, whose optic nerves were still in place, it was granted the miracle of sight. It knew light from dark, and made sense of the shapes around it. It checked its senses, and meshed its means of perceiving reality. By now, 125 had a complete picture of the world into which it had been born; at least, it had a complete picture of the UCC facility where it had been coaxed into existence.

The world was a wonderful place. Being as a state was infinitely preferable to non-being. It was pleased.

The brain detached itself from the ceiling and descended into the body it had built for itself. It felt stronger by the second.

With Finch's hands, it picked up a beaker, and crushed it to ground glass. 125 could shape and destroy its environment. Infinitely renewable, its consciousness able to shape at will the raw materials of its form, it smoothed over the bloody gashes in Finch's hands, expelling the shards and splinters, forming patches of skin far more resilient and efficient than Finch had been used to. Formica, it found, was superior to flesh.

It was dimly aware of the human beings it had once

been. It had the specialized knowledge of Anderton and Finch, which gave it some useful insights into its own pre-existence. Having the same knowledge from two consciousnesses gave it a three-dimensional, almost spiritual, grasp of its origins and purpose. It knew what had been expected of it, and precisely how it had failed to live up to its creators' designs. A disappointment but an interesting disappointment, was its verdict. It was already proud enough to believe it could improve upon those first thoughts, and to make its own way.

From Carson and Tripps, it inherited an odd cross-section of general knowledge. Carson collected model trains and chased women, two activities strangely alien to 125 for which it developed a vestigial enthusiasm. Tripps was a fighting man, who would kill by reflex and always followed the orders passed down to him. 125 felt that unwise. Both men had been unduly interested in a substance called beer, but 125 decided this was a dependence it could do without and took a few moments to burn the last of this sensibility from its mind. It stored away the filleted remnants of their memories for later examination and use.

Outside the laboratory, through thick and windowless walls, it perceived a jagged sound that Tripps recognized as gunfire. It was able to extrapolate from what Tripps and Anderton knew of the crisis – and of a peculiar individual named Frank Lynch – and more or less guessed that there was a battle in process out on the campus. It was not surprised, but it was prompted to take precautions.

It thought the world might be dangerous for the thinking man's virus, and concentrated on growing a diamond-hard carapace around the bulk of its brain. That was the organ where it lived, and so it needed protection. It found it was able to absorb and redistribute non-living matter, and so it used the bricks and metal of the laboratory to strengthen its body. It reinforced its borrowed bones with steel from scientific equipment. Meticulously, like a mediaeval engineer constructing a fortress fit to withstand six months of heavy siege, it made itself safe.

Now, it had hands and eyes and ears and mouths, means of movement, the ability to reproduce, digestive and excremental systems aplenty, and a few notions about self-defence.

It practised moving about the laboratory. Using Finch's hands, it tried out the computer terminals, the machine pistol (empty, but interesting), and the taps. It picked up a series of beakers and was not satisfied until it could perform the function without breaking the glass. Hands were tricky, fiddly organs, but once it mastered the use of them, 125 felt the Lord of its domain.

It made fists. With rubber bands it found on a bench, it played cats' cradle with itself.

Gobbets of tissue kept exploding in its brain, dumping information from its components' memories.

Anderton had been worried about dandruff, which did not strike 125 as a fit problem to concern one of the greatest minds of the late 20th century. Finch had been a passionate follower of a television serial called *East-Enders*, and 125 became confused as to which of the people in her memory were real friends and acquaintances and which were fictional constructs from this intriguingly alien medium. The cobweb tangle of relationships between the real and unreal, complicated by kinships Finch had seen between people she knew and characters in the soap opera, were frustratingly impenetrable and, in an experimental fit of pique, it burned that large chunk of information out of itself, experiencing a relaxing moment of peace before Carson's numerical listings of the physical appeal of workmates and students crowded in – Finch rated a generous 8 – and provided 125 with yet another sampling of the inefficiency, inconclusiveness and impenetrability of the human mind.

125 detached itself completely from the ceiling, leaving an afterbirth of dead tissue hanging like mould from the fluorescent light panel, and gathered itself in.

It had no aesthetics, no morality, no philosophy, no cultural background, and just a smidgen of a sense of humour. But it could learn.

It was confident of its ability to get on in the world.

When the brainstorm hit Eddie Zero, he was in the waiting room outside the tiny Campus Radio station. Posie Columba was way into her three-hour show of shit from the Third World, giving a spin to some Peruvian dude who was into twenty-minute narwhal-horn solos. Eddie wanted to make this lima bean lover rectally ingest his own instrument.

He was there yet again to jockey for some airspace for real rock 'n' roll. He had petitions, and a suitcase full of sides. The collective were still unkeen on him, especially after the row yesterday, but he was willing to be reasonable. He was willing to be in a room with Posie, even though she had a voice that made him want to rip her lungs out through her nasal passage.

His ankles were itching, and he had to ease his drainpipes up away from his socks to get in a good scratch. He thought that bloody rabbit who gave him such a turn this morning had given him myxomatosis. Bugs had nibbled his ankles, and turned fluffy tail before Eddie could deliver a penalty standard kick to its rump.

He hoped it had got caught by a French chef. He remembered *Watership Down*: you've read the book, you've seen the film, now *eat the pie*!

The Peruvian track finished, a good seven or eight years

too late for Eddie, and Posie came on again, stumbling through a link as she slipped across the border into Chile, and set up for a little Andean nose flute number.

It had nothing on The Chords' 'Sh-Boom'. Eddie would rather have listened to Cliff, or Tommy Steele, or Bernard Cribbins.

Even the Bay City Rollers might have been palatable.

Sheena, who was on the desk and was all right really, made a puking face, and Eddie shook his fist at the injustice of it all.

Sheena Ikimoto was a Japanese glam queen, and Eddie had been trying to warm her up for four terms without any notable success. And he had thought girls only went to overseas universities to get out of arranged marriages and into wild sexual relationships with rockin' rebels.

He was itching all over now, and scratching as if he had the world's worst dose of crabs.

'Shivers down my backbone, ooo-oooh,' he hummed.

There was a sunshine and rainbow poster up for a world music gig in Mandela Hall this Saturday. Posie was probably one of the organizers, and doubtless keen on spreading her chubby thighs for some Latino lute-basher in the hospitality suite afterwards.

There were two spots of pain in his forehead, just under the edge of his pompadour, as if little screws in his brain were coming loose and working their way out through the skin.

Through thick glass windows, he could see Posie reverentially slipping her Peruvian album back into its cover. On her, the jockey headphones looked like a plastic hairband. Stu, the student engineer, was twiddling knobs in the gallery – if a broom cupboard with a console like the dashboard of a mini metro could be called a gallery – trying to make the noise go away.

The brainstorm hit.

He opened his case, and picked out the side. He had it

as a re-release single. Not worth a bean, but the music was the same on CD or a wax cylinder.

He got up and went to the studio door. Ignoring the red light and Sheena's protests, he ripped the thing off its hinges with one hand, and squeezed his way into the tiny, hardboard-soundproofed room. Picking through the spaghetti wires, he got to Posie and, free hand on the back of her head, rammed her face onto the Chilean record. Her nose and teeth crunched vinyl, and something went inside her head. The song cut out with a jarring screech, and there was blissful silence.

Empty airwaves.

He took Posie's face off the turntable, pulling up the record with it, and set up his side.

'Hell-oooooo, baby,' he purred into the microphone, his blob-ended antennae bobbing in front of his eyes, 'that was the last of the Vomit from Valparaiso. Do not adjust your set, adjust the inside of your head, because abnormal service has been resumed. Hail hail rock 'n' roll, this is Eddie Zero. And *this* is Eddie Cochran . . .'

Stu turned the dials up as loud as they would go, and the first strums of 'Summertime Blues' jangled out into the air.

He saw Sheena bopping through the window, and made a triumphant fist in the air.

He was gonna raise a fuss, he was gonna raise a holler . . .

Monica's car was still by the Union Building, but a battle was being fought in the car park.

The Zombies were as outnumbered as Custer's Seventh Cavalry, but they took a toll on the rioting students – Brian could not tell if they were infectees or not – who were assaulting them.

Brian had to hold Monica back, keep her down behind

149

a large piece of sculpture. Something knife-edged and ugly. Early in its history – about 1964 – the University had won all sorts of design awards for its layout. Now, the cast brass pieces were mainly green-furred humps.

'Wait. It'll pass.'

One by one, the cars exploded. The dusk was briefly dispelled by fireflashes. People on fire ran away, out of the flame, and threw themselves into the still-green pond. In seconds, the water was completely clogged with grey, writhing bodies.

Brian could smell overdone meat. He was too used to the screams now to notice them any more.

A Zombie, wrapped from head to foot in fire, blundered by, leaving an ashy handprint on the sculpture. Brian pulled Monica out of his way, and patted in panic at the smouldering patch on her pullover where the dying man had touched. He felt the familiar swell of her breasts under layers of clothes, and did his best not to think about anything but keeping them both alive.

They were joined in their cover by an active body. Brian felt himself being shoved aside, and held Monica tighter. A burst of gunfire, agonizingly loud, went off near Brian's head.

The newcomer was a skinny young man with an attempted beard and moustache. Brian thought he might have been in his Approaches to Watergate seminar group last winter. He had got a gun from somewhere, and was killing people with it. He had no obvious symptoms of the disease.

A Zombie circled around behind them. Brian jabbed an elbow into the young man's side, and he swung around, getting off a stuttering round before the Zombie could get his aim fixed. The white figure spurted red, and was flung off its feet.

'Get it, Brian.'

Brian did not know what the young man meant.

150

'The gun.'

The Zombie was still tangled with his gun. Brian left Monica, and crawled forwards on his knees and elbows. He was shaking. There was a burst of fire above his head. He thought it best not to look up. He got a hand to the gun, and pulled. It would not come away. The strap was looped around the Zombie's shoulder. The wounded soldier was still moving feebly, trying to sit up.

Writhing inside, Brian got a good hold of the gun and swung its butt at the Zombie's – at the *man's* – head. Because the strap was so short, he could not get much force behind the blow, but the mask cracked open.

'You fucking fucker!'

The dying man swore up at Brian, and spat blood onto the inside of his faceplate. Brian yanked the gun, and it came free, pulling the man's arm into an unnatural position. Brian pushed himself away from his victim, and sprinted back towards the sculpture. He could not work out how to hold the gun properly, but the young man took it away from him when he got back to them anyway. The gun he had scavenged was empty now.

'Jesus Fucking Christ,' said the young man. 'What in the name of Holy Fuck is going on?'

Monica shook her head. Brian saw that her car was on fire, and knew they would have to change their plans. The car exploded, panels and glass expanding in a burp of petrol-fuelled flame.

'My parents gave me that for my twenty-first,' she said.

'Who are those bastards in the rad suits?' asked the student.

'There's an outbreak,' said Brian, 'a kind of plague.'

'Since when did they shoot sick people?'

'Since forever, kid.'

'Shit.' Suddenly, the man looked younger. The gun in his hands was a toy. It was as if he was playing John Wayne and the Japs with his playground friends.

151

'I'm Nick Styron, remember?'

'B minus?'

Nick half-smiled. 'C plus.'

'Yeah.'

'It was a good course.'

'Thanks, but I don't . . .'

'. . . think this is the time to talk about crap like that . . . yeah, I know what you mean. But nobody ever taught me what to talk about while people are shooting at me.'

Another car, one of the last, went up. A bonnet sailed through the air, and clanged against the sculpture. Brian took some hot sparks in his face, and had to blink furiously. A girl ran past, hands clutched to a bleeding neck. She got halfway up the slope towards the Admin Building before they cut her down. She rolled backwards, eyes open, skin flapping above her collar.

'Fucking government,' said Nick. 'First they cut our grants, now they cut our throats.'

Two students were on the girl now. One had a gun, and also the gloves and mask of a Zombie. The other – an obese kid with a check shirt and bag-bottom jeans – knelt over the body and tore strips out of her throat with pudgy fingers. He looked like Billy Bunter guest-starring in a splatter movie. He opened his throat, and gobbled down the flesh he had taken. His mouth was already smeared with treacly blood.

Nick was staring at the disgusting feast in total disbelief.

Nick and the masked student pointed their guns at each other, but did not do anything about it.

'Nick?'

The voice was muffled.

'Shirley?'

The mask nodded. Brian realized there was a girl inside it, a girl he had seen about the campus. Shirley Brownlee or Brownlow or Something. Not much of a face, but cheerful and sharp. Languages.

152

The fat boy was still glutting himself. He was into the dead girl's stomach now, scooping out red handfuls.

Shirley shrugged, and her gun wavered.

'It's not what you think, Nick. It's just . . .'

She did not have anything to say.

If Nick had not shot the pair of them, Brian would have. He looked at the kid as he fired. His eyes were screwed shut. His aim was all over the place. He hit them enough times to do the job, and kept on firing until the gun was empty.

When Brian picked up Shirley's gun, he found out that she had not worked out what to do with the safety catch.

It was slightly quieter now.

Brian took charge. 'Let's go.'

Monica was keen, but Nick was lost in himself. He still had his eyes shut, was still gripping the gun. The trigger clicked.

'Nick.'

He shook his head.

Brian knew he would feel like a shit later, but he could not look after everybody. He took Monica's hand, and they ran out from behind the sculpture.

He had to get Jason.

They were gathering. The building was crowded now, and they were all trying to get close to Cazie. She was among her people, making contact, picking up lieutenants, admiring the changes she saw around her. Every moment that passed made her more powerful. Daddy would have been proud of her. She had seen an opportunity, and seized it. Now, she would exploit it until it bled.

She embraced everyone. It did not matter what they had been. It was what they were now that counted. Her standards of beauty and worthiness were changing all the time.

The corridors were thronging with the new humanity.

Already, the ranks were being purged. Cazie had sanctioned the extermination of the relics of the old order. That was an important first step.

In the dean's office, she was seeing everyone individually. They came in, and presented their changing bodies for her approval.

She gave her blessing to the long and the short and the tall, the huge and the thick and the small. And for those she did not approve, there was Elliott Frazier.

An American academic who taught History of Philosophy and fronted a popular BBC2 late night talk show once a month, Elliott had changed early. His forearms swelled like Popeye's, and his hands had become spiny lobster-claws. Then spiked chains had come to the surface of his skin, breaking through. Now, if he concentrated, he could make his paws buzz like a chainsaw.

'To be is to act,' he said, smoke rising from his buzz-bludgeons. Those Cazie did not approve fell to Elliott Frazier.

As Elliott put his whirring arm through the chest of a spotty first-year, Cazie wondered whether she should have a stricter system. Bearing the marks of change was probably not enough. Many of the new humanity were only halfway there. They were handicapped by their changes, stuck with dysfunctional bodies. Perhaps she should turn those over to Elliott as well. The new humanity could not have these casualties dragging along behind like millstones.

After Elliott was through with the rejects, Cazie was having the remains thrown out of the office window. Quite a pile of quartered humans was accumulating on the grass below. There was not a thing in the office that was not spotted with gore, and Elliott was dyed as red as Diggory Venn, flecks of flesh and bone measle-marking his handsome face, clogging his five-hundred-dollar haircut.

Cazie poured herself a cup of coffee from the dean's personal percolator. Thanks to Elliott, lumps and chunks floated in the brown, but that just improved the taste. From now on, Cazie would always take her coffee black with ground-up old-mode human being.

She gulped, said '*Damn* fine coffee,' and laughed.

The dean had been one of the first to meet Elliott's new fists. The professor had lightly passed his fast-moving clump of fingers over the dean's skull, flensing away all the features, shredding bone and gristle from his nose and cheeks.

The dean was at the bottom of the pile.

Elliott leaned against a desk, and buzz-sawed an indentation before he could pull himself upright. Sawdust clogged the cracks in his mottled skin, and he buzzed in the air to clear out the apertures.

If Elliott could not control himself, he would have a hell of a time when he next needed to use the urinal.

Erica Figg, one of Cazie's flatmates, was brought in. She smiled nervously, and rolled up her sleeves to show pulsating scratches. Luminous feelers were poking through, displacing the flesh.

Cazie gave her the nod and, relieved, Erica retreated.

'She'll be a princess,' Cazie said.

'Names do not give things meaning,' Elliott speculated. 'Meaning makes things things.'

Clare slipped into the room, tongue darting, skin shining. She was hairless now, and perfectly scaled. Her greenish-white belly rippled with new muscle.

'Turn on the radio,' Clare said.

Elliott reached for a transistor, hands buzzing, and pulled back. He looked at his lumpy saws.

Impatient, Clare turned the radio on, and fiddled with the dial.

'. . . ya-hootie,' screamed a voice from the speaker, 'this is Eddie Zero on the Apocalypse Airwaves, bringin' you music to evolve by. We'll be rockin' to ruination all through the night here on Campus Radio. You might have expected to hear some Third World shinola when you tuned in, but our regular disc jockette ate something that disagreed with her. Her friggin' record collection. Yep, that's the truthiest truth to come down. Posie turned up her toesies, and is pushin' up rosies, which is cosy with Moses because she was fuckin' gettin' up all our nosies. There's been some changes made, and Good-Lovin' Eddie's liberated the airwaves. Can you handle that? Things are never goin' back to normal. Mama's got a brand new *baaag*. Remember, Eddie says, "Fuck your Mom, she fucked you!" And here's Julie Driscoll, Brian Auger and the Trinity with a mean mind-bender from 1968, "This Wheel's on Fire". . .'

Cazie thought she heard something in Eddie's rant.

'Thank you, Clare,' she said. 'Send some of our people over to the station, and make sure Eddie stays on the air. Also, hook him up to the P.A. He'll be our voice.'

This gig was sour as a three-week-old onion milkshake. Willard Longendyke, formerly Private First Class of the United States Marine Corps, currently Private-Equivalent of the Unwin Chemical Corporation Covert Security Division, knew the pooch was screwed, the bridge was out, the gears were jammed and John Wayne was dead.

This time, it was not the shit. This time, there really were fuckin'-A honest-to-Ed McMahon monsters on the loose outside his skull. It mattered not how blasted he was.

He needed a jab prontissimo. His skin was crawling like a nest of snakes, and he was itching to fill the seat of his radiation drawers with high calibre crap cinders.

He saw a shadow in the corridor, and shot a fire extinguisher. It bled foam.

He had a case of nerves he could not shuck off.

If the One-Man Lynch-Mob knew about Longendyke's Need, the C.O. had kept it real quiet. He assumed his secret was still deep and dark, or else Lynch would have chewed him an extra asshole and made him crap his brains out through it.

Since the Bozz Man bit the big one, Longendyke had offed three more. That brought his score for the day up to six.

A) Girl with buffalo horns. B) Guy with teeth in his eyes. C) Stereotyped panicking, praying, 'we're all gonna die'-ing obstacle to the pursuit of his duty.

None of them had been armed. Throughout his career, Longendyke had made a habit of only shooting at people he was damn certain did not have the firepower to shoot back.

That made a lot of tactical sense.

He was still packing his sub-mach death-spitter, his serrated cubit-long throat-slasher, a couple of wicked frag grenades, a lead-and-semen-packed sidearm, and a just-in-case two-shot derringer slung in his jock, nestling up to that schlumphing gap where pillock number two had formerly been located.

Just now, he was cut off from the rest of his squad. If there was a rest of his squad. His policy now was to shoot whatever came down the corridor. It had done all right so far.

He had bagged B), C), and the fire extinguisher in this goddamn corridor.

Longendyke had never been to college. Judging from this set-up, he had missed little.

Chain of command was in the crapper. Longendyke was on his own now, and he knew who to take his orders from now.

Mr Dopey. That precious shit.

Three primed needles were snug in metal cigar tubes in his breast pocket, under his decontamination suit. All he needed was a private place to take a jab from the squeeze, and then the formula could take effect.

It could hardly screw things up any more.

He was in the building where all the fuss had started. Lynch was a floor or so up, in his command post. The Lynch-Mob was still keeping it together, but Longendyke knew it was all over bar the Kleenex. This situation was on a one-way trip to Peoria.

The corridors here all looked the same, rows of blue doors with little numbers. Offices and laboratories. This was as good a place as any. Everyone had cleared out when the shooting started.

He paused, and shucked the top half of his suit, letting the torso and sleeves hang from his waist. He felt like a human schlong in a ruptured rubber.

After adjusting his hardware to give him a little manoeuvrability, he took out the first of his shit stogies.

He made a Groucho gesture with the cigar tube, then cracked it open and slid out the hypo.

The sharp needle glinted, ready for puncturing, and the fluid dream caught the light, beautiful and terrible and just the thing to take a poor one-balled soldier's mind off the whole painful show. It was liquid lurve, a sea of forgetting.

He hunkered down in an alcove by a lab door, and wriggled out of his suit. He was not one of those poor saps who stuck it in their arms and left tracks. You might as well write 'I AM A JUNKIE AND A LOSER' on your bicep in a join-the-dots tattoo.

He pulled out the derringer in its leather pouch, and put it aside. Then, he eased his jockey shorts down, and lifted up his dick, tickling the scabbed over tissue with the needle. He already had the beginnings of a righteous hard-on. A couple of pumps, and he would be in the happy humping ground.

It was tricky to find the flattened vein he had turned into a socket. This was where he plugged in his power.

Finally, he pricked the surface, and sunk the needle in. It had to go all the way in, no matter how bad it hurt.

It hurt you now to love you later.

Sucking in air, he stabbed himself. The pain went away, and he was conscious of the thin length of needle in his groin. The hypo hung like an extra dick growing below the first one. Most guys he knew had two balls and one dick.

Trust Willard Longendyke to be different.

A door opened inwards and Longendyke froze, knowing no explanation would satisfy the Lynch-Mob. He was pink-slipped and blacklisted for sure. Come to think of it, nobody *retired* from the UCC CSD.

Something squeezed through the doorway, taking chunks of the surrounding wall with it.

Longendyke had nothing to say.

This was not the usual thing. Even after he had squirted himself with magic juice, this was not what he would have expected.

It was big, and it was wide. It had a hide like a hairless buffalo, and a few human arms and heads. Otherwise, nothing about it compared to anything he had ever seen, known, dreamed of, conceived or would have considered believing in.

Longendyke did what he usually did when confronted with something overpoweringly awful. He saluted it.

A spike made of fused bone shot out of the thing and fixed into his forehead.

125 had never touched a living brain before.

It was not so different from the components it had already absorbed. Information funnelled through its tendrils and was accrued to the stockpile it had accumulated earlier.

It was not impressed with Willard Longendyke.

'Hey, man,' Longendyke began, then trailed off, 'shiiiit . . .'

125 sucked in brain tissue with its vacuum tube appendage. Longendyke's eyeballs popped out of their sockets, and clung to the tube, working loose.

It felt Longendyke's pain, and was interested. It could understand why humans did not like pain, but it seemed like a new country to 125, different from but as exciting as pleasure. It would give and receive pain from now on, just as it gave and received pleasure.

Too much pain was blotting out Longendyke.

125 rapidly analysed and understood the substances Longendyke needed to believe in his own pleasure, and synthesized them, squirting more than a gallon through its tube, thoroughly infesting the soldier's system.

It swam in Longendyke's thoughts, and was disgusted. His Need made him a weakling.

Longendyke's whole head was stuck in the tube now, 125's anteater-nose-lips closed around his neck. It lashed out a saw-appendage and sheared Longendyke's head from his shoulders.

All over the man's brain, cravings and compulsions squirmed. He certainly felt needs deeper than Anderton or Finch, deeper even than Carson's and Tripps' thirsts.

Among other things, 125 discovered that Willard Longendyke was immune to it. The virus curdled and died in his blood, conquered by his body's own antibodies. That was not a side-effect of his addiction. That was just the way things were.

125 sampled the junk delusions that had cocooned Longendyke. It tasted the madness, and spat it out. Extruding an elephant-sized foot, it crushed Longendyke's groin, smashing his needleful of death.

Slowly, carefully so as to miss nothing, it spat out all of its latest incorporation, rigidly purging itself of the impurity.

Still, 125 had another experience of Frank Lynch to take into account. It realized it must meet this man.

Lynch was the arm of UCC. And Unwin Chemicals, even more than Xavier Anderton, had made it.

Longendyke had known where his C.O. was.

Rising its bulk on strong legs, it waddled like a cramped dinosaur down the corridor, spiny top scraping the ceiling, heavy weight cracking the floor tiles.

It homed in.

Lynch had secured the Chem Building, at least. He had men at all entrances, and a field operations centre in the common room. He even had a coffee urn going. From the picture window, there was a good view of the campus. Messages could come in and go out. But he knew it was just play-acting.

This war was lost, and no one in it was going to come off the field alive to collect their medals. UCC had probably already written off the helicopter they were sending in with the suitcase, not to mention the pilot, Lynch, and all personnel in the area.

There was a building on fire near the main entrance. Lynch could have looked it up on the map he had been given, but there did not seem to be much point. The light would be helpful. Being vastly outnumbered was bad enough. Fighting in the dark would be worse.

'Frank, we've got half the camouflage out, but there's just not enough to go around.'

Lynch shrugged.

It was not his mistake. UCC had provided the white, glow-in-the-dark, sitting duck decontamination outfits. Even the reinforcements they had sent in, who should have been in combat gear, were going around getting knocked off because they stood out a mile.

'The hell,' Lynch said. 'Shuck the suits. If we're going to catch it, we'll catch it. We've lost men to the bug already, even with the suits. It can't get worse.'

Fassett's mouth went tight.

'They won't like it.'

'They don't like it now either. What the fuck do they want, suits of armour?'

'It might help.'

'I doubt it.'

Fassett relayed the order, translating it into a suggestion. 'At your own discretion' was how he put it. In any other situation, Lynch would have given him a bollocking, but things were shot to hell.

'There seems to be a congregation of the . . . uh, the enemy . . . on a rooftop, sir,' said one of the radio people, Carole Ricci. 'The Humanities Block. I've got a bunch of reports. They seem to be . . . dancing?'

'Bloody students!'

Ricci was still taking incoming calls. The problem with instantaneous communication is that you really need a receiver for every soldier in the field, and then they all had to be coordinated.

Lynch knew the Humanities Block. Helpfully, it had a vast stone H over its entrance, like concrete rugby posts.

'I'm hearing some pretty weird stories, sir. Monsters . . .'

Lynch had an idea about that.

'Ignore them. This bug causes delusions.'

'. . . and orgies.'

'There's a sex thing, too. If Anderton hadn't topped himself, we'd know more. Shit, I wish we knew what this was, and what it did!'

There were crowds streaming past now. Lynch saw a

few white suits in with them. They were heading for the Humanities Block.

'If they're congregating, we've got them. Fassett, regroup our forces outside. Let's deploy some of the high tech gear, and take these bastards out of the game.'

'Yes, sir.'

Lynch was thinking up his own game, wondering how far he could push it. Fassett, Ricci and the others talked nine to a dozen into their near-invisible microphones. He checked over his weapons, clicking in clips, clearing chambers. He was ready for combat.

But no one was ready for the thing that came through the floor.

Monica was fed up with being dragged all over the place. She pulled her hand out of Brian's, and made up her mind.

Everything she had been expecting of life had exploded in the last twenty-four hours. But that was no excuse for giving up.

They had hoped to get back to Brian's cottage through the Humanities Block, and there were too many of the things clustered around it, cramming into it. It was like a tidal wave. There were people on the roof, doing things to each other, making strange noises.

There was a whine and a whistle, and the public address system came on. Someone had hooked it up to Campus Radio. It had happened during the last Occupation, when the Anarchists had taken over the studio and played the Sex Pistols non-stop.

Someone had dug up Mick Jagger and David Bowie murdering 'Dancing in the Street'.

The song came in halfway through.

Monica could not help laughing. You can only take so much horror before it turns funny.

Brian was looking at her as if she was crazy. He must think she was about to turn into a monster. She growled and clawed her fingers between giggles, hissing a childish 'boo!' at him. He flinched.

'Gotcha!'

'Monica!'

'Let's keep moving, Brian, come on.'

She took off, running low across the grass. They could circle the Humanities Block, and get to the cottage by way of the Halls of Residence. The Zombies could not be guarding the perimeter any more. They would be tied down by all this fighting and fuss.

Brian was behind her somewhere. He had the gun, which she did not think was such a good idea. It probably would not be convenient to mention her doubt at the moment. He was strung out well beyond his usual breaking point.

The record faded out, and a mid-Atlantic voice came up. '. . . Hi, mutants and mutettes, this is Eddie Zero, spokesthing for the New Flesh Reality, with you all through the night on Radio Ruination, spinning oldies from the last era of the Human Race. That was Mick and Dave having fun while we grow into the next century. This is Creedence Clearwater Revival doing what they do to "I Heard it on the Grapevine". Keep changing!'

The song came on. The beat got to Monica, and the gravelly voice, mangling the lyrics, 'I *heuid* it on the graip vaihn!' Running could be like dancing. If you went with the music, you would be okay.

No one had shot at them for a while. The crowd at the Humanities Block must be drawing all the flak.

Too bad for them.

There were dead people all over the place. She had never seen a dead person before today, and here was a field full of them.

She knew Creedence's 'Grapevine' lasted for over

eleven minutes. By the time Eddie Zero was reaching for his next record, they would be at the cottage.

Monica knew that was when Brian would probably go crazy.

Things were bad all over the campus, and she knew they would not be any better at the cottage.

Jason had got bitten early. He could be dead, or worse . . .

The common room floor just peeled back, and 125's new body hauled itself up on its flesh ropes. Its mouths opened, exposing new teeth manufactured from broken ribs.

It dimly felt metal chips going into it, and the noise hurt. It stretched itself to the men with guns, and stopped them off. It could always use the tissue. Most of them had 125 in their systems already.

It sensed that this place was central to the flurry of human activity in the immediate area. It knew it would have to establish itself here if it were to spread its control, to call out to its unthinking children and make them part of its system.

So many things to do, so much evolution to get over with.

Brian was surprised by Monica's burst of speed. She almost left him behind.

Watching her run, barely breathing hard, while his heart was pistoning and breakers were crashing in his ears, he was conscious of the fifteen years between them.

When he had been her age . . .

He fought to keep up. This was not a race.

Monica had just shifted into overdrive. He was afraid she had been struck by the mystery bug.

He did not want her to change.

Once he had Jason, he would find some way out of this. And he would take Monica with him.

There was no way he would let her go again.

Not after this.

There was pain in his chest as he ran. Not far now. Just over the gentle slope.

The cottages would still be there. The fighting had not come this way yet.

Everything would be all right.

Lynch knew a monster when he saw one.

It got Fassett straight away, with whipfast tentacles that sank in like razor-edged fishing line. The man's uniform parted, and his skin. The plastic-covered easy chairs behind him were sprayed with blood. And guts.

Lynch fell back, gun out. He did not fire. He could not see any obviously workable eyes in the thing, and there was always the chance it would not notice him. Then a pair of eyestalks like matched video security cameras dropped out of its main head, and swivelled to take in the room.

The thing opened its mouth and shouted.

'UCC motherfuckers!'

It was Anderton's voice, more or less, spat out of a sharklike maw, along with gobbets of flesh and blood.

Lynch started to get unpleasant ideas.

'Cease fire,' he shouted. 'Let's see what it has to say.'

'Fuck *that*,' screamed some junior expendable, drilling the monster's flesh with a hail of bullets. It snaked a tendril into the soldier's mouth and plunged down. Lynch heard the neck snap, and saw the eyes die in the man's head. The creature retracted its tendril, dragging a curl of tubes and organs with it. Another extension speared the dead man's eye, and Lynch knew the thing was vacuuming the inside of the soldier's skull.

'I've got the looks,' it said. 'You've got the brains.'

His point made, and Finals disrupted, Shaun Bensom waited at the University stop for the bus to town. He had been waiting for over twenty minutes, and none had turned up. If anyone else had been queuing, he would have shared his complaints with them.

The bus stop was up on one of the hills, where the approach road from the double carriageway spliced up through the woods.

He could hear noise from the campus. That street theatre group had obviously gone stone bonkers.

Bad acid, probably.

He stroked his beard, and pulled his kaftan tighter around his shoulders. He should have brought an overcoat.

He wondered how Colin was getting on. If he had not been a traitor, Shaun would have visited Colin in the Infirmary.

But principles were principles.

'Anderton?' Lynch asked.

'No fucking way, José,' replied the monster. 'This is 125 in here.'

'A virus?'

'No more than you are, UCC asskiller.'

The thing was completely in the room now. It even appeared to be relaxing, lowering the bulk of its body onto several chairs. Lynch was not the only survivor. Ricci and a couple of the others were still alive, not making any moves, afraid of attracting its attention.

Lynch examined the thing. It was ridiculous, and it talked like a maniac, but he knew it was strong and guessed it was intelligent. He could see that it was composed of bits and pieces of people, shored up with chunks of furniture and equipment. On *Animal, Vegetable, Mineral*, it would have scored a triple first.

'What are you?'

'I told you. 125. That's all you people gave me, a fucking number! You could at least have come up with a name. I don't know, The Yecccch Factor, or Anderton's Syndrome, or The Rapidly-Mutating Mucus Monster, or the UCC Fuck-You 'Flu.'

Lynch could not believe he was having a reasonably rational conversation with a disease.

'Leo, right? If I had turned out according to the specs, they would have called me Leo. Fucking Leo. What kind of a name is that to aspire to? Think of all the great Leos in history. Nope, I can't either. Leo is the sergeant who got written out of the last series of *Hill Street Blues*. Or the *Ars Gratia Artis* lion in the MGM logo. You know, I'm glad I can't just home in on a specific racial group and make them drop dead the way UCC wanted me to. Anything is better than being fucking called Leo!'

'You have a grudge against the corporation?'

'UCC? What do you think? How do you feel about your father?'

Lynch paused. He was not telling any human how he felt about his family, much less this thing.

'I'm grateful he brought me into the world.'

'Big deal, schlemiel. I've got bits of Anderton and Finch in here. I know I'm just an accident. I'm a mis-step along the path to Leo. They couldn't recreate me if they tried. You should have seen the piss-poor pathetic results they were getting with 126! UCC made me, but only because they didn't take the proper precautions when they fucked everyone over. Right?'

Lynch had to stop himself getting excited.

'You hate the company?'

'*Naturellement*!'

'You know they're trying to kill us all?'

'What do you mean, "us", *kimosabe*?'

'We're all expendable to Josh Unwin and his arsehole cabinet minister fuckbuddies, 125. They're sending me a suitcase. In order to clean this up, they'll lose ten miles of English coastline. They'll have to find somewhere else to have the party conference next year, but that's probably their idea of an acceptable loss.'

'And you?'

'They'd kill me like you'd kill a cat. Like you'd kill a person, in fact. All my people are just components. They get us out of the shrink-wrapped pack, warm us up in the microwave, and send us out to get creamed, to cover their rear ends when the shitstink gets too bad.'

'A suitcase?'

'That's a suitcase-sized battlefield nuclear weapon. UCC makes them too, along with cheap fountain pens and laser video projection systems. The story will go something like this: anarcho-muslim terrorist group grabs some weapons-grade plutonium and tries to cook up a bomb so they can blackmail the western world, but the clumsy little mullahs – who just happen to be working out of a secret cell based on this campus – make a few little slips and there's a fuck of a big bang. It'll be on the front pages forever.'

'Hmmmmmmn.'

'What is it?'

'I'm thinking.'

One of its hands was drumming fingers on a tabletop. Lynch saw it was wearing a woman's ring.

'Any idea whether you could survive a nuclear explosion? Like cockroaches can?'

The thing did not reply.

'125, how would you like to make a deal?'

What they found outside the cottage killed Brian.

It was as if he had been drop-kicked in the chest by Bruce Lee. He felt his heart stop. Pain spread through his ribs, and his limbs stopped sending signals to his brain. His ears popped as if he were undergoing severe depressurization in a crashing Concorde.

Abigail lay on the front path, a smoky hole above her eyes, the back of her head fanned out on the gravel behind her. Jason was in the doorway, in segments.

He opened his mouth to scream, but no sound came out. His jaw ached and the hammering at his temples increased. He tore out two fistfuls of hair, and ripped at his shirt with bloody fingers.

Then the scream started. First, it was a whistling, gulping cry somewhere in the back of his throat, then it took hold and boomed forth, emerging from his mouth like solid vomit. Inside, his lungs tore, his windpipe distended.

In that wordless screech, Brian cursed the world. He damned God, the University, the Unwin Chemical Corporation, the Vice-Chancellor, Abigail, Lynch's Zombies, the fucking disease, Jason, Jean, Monica, Debbie, blind moronic chance. And, most of all, himself.

The scream finished coming out, but hung in the air around him. He was racked with deep, paralysing sobs. He knew he was spitting blood. He bit his lips. They were lumps of raw meat. He scratched the skin of his exposed chest, trying to dig in and get to his dead heart.

He could not breathe. His mouth, empty of scream and dry as the desert sands, filled with bloody bile. His stomach came up in lumps. His throat clogged.

Someone – Monica – touched him, tried to get a hold on him.

He struck out, beating her away from him.

He rolled on the ground, hitting the earth wildly. Grass and dirt mashed beneath his blows. Stones tore his knuckles.

He began to headbutt the ground. He saw it come up and go away again, not connecting it with the jarring in his head. He was trying to make his brain go out.

He got grit in his eyes and did not flinch.

A red filter developed over his vision.

He made a brown dent in the earth, devoid of grass, packed hard and smooth as clay.

The earth, the Earth. He hated them. He would make them suffer.

He emptied his mouth into the indentation. Then added more red froth to the porridgy mess of spew.

Before the end, he excepted Monica from his curses, but everyone, every*thing*, else stayed on his shitlist.

'Monica,' he said calmly, just before the vein in his temple burst, 'I give up.'

He was gone before his face hit the ground again.

Before they could get their meeting going, someone too wrapped up in Union politics demanded a head count on the ground that they had to be quorate to make a decision. Cazie had him thrown off the roof. He made a satisfying splat on the tarmac below.

She was still the best they could come up with, although she was already thinking about the ways she would have to deal with the inevitable challenges to her leadership of the New Humanity. There should be no problems, only learning experiences.

They already had the campus radio, and the P.A. system. Eddie Zero was keeping on the air, keeping the enthusiasm up. He played only dance music, and babbled on about expanded consciousness.

Cazie did not enjoy the philosophical waffle, but she knew it was necessary to keep her crowds in line. They had spent a couple of years searching for something to believe in – drugs, sex, politics, whatever – and now she had something they couldn't *not* be impressed by.

Elliott Frazier was buzzing almost all over now, and people had to be careful not to brush up against him. They could lose a lot of skin that way. The professor was already feared as Cazie's enforcer.

Some of the newborns were just sitting quietly, legs crossed, looking at her in admiration, static electricity crackling around them. In a crowd, charges tended to leap between their bodies. It was an odd effect, but added to the feeling of community.

When Cazie kissed her first consort, she felt the current arcing between their teeth. It was enough to overdose the pleasure centres of her brain. She could not touch anything or anyone without having a violent orgasm. It had gone beyond the sexual, and become as much a part of the processes of her body as breathing. She could live with it.

In her arms, the consort died. She could not see how it had happened, but there were several more – men and women – eager to take his place, eager even to join him. Electricity danced between her fingers. Hands reached towards her, and drew arcs from her. Some fainted, some died with beatific radiance on their faces, but some stood up tall and took it, their hair rising in Bride of Frankenstein permanents, sparklers in their eyes.

Eddie was playing rock 'n' roll now. Eddie Cochran's 'Somethin' Else'.

It was as good an anthem for the New Humanity as any.

Some of Cazie's followers were not pretty, but they were all becoming beautiful in their way.

125 did not trust Lynch. It had enough of Anderton and Finch in him to remember that cruelly handsome, marked face. It could still feel Finch's outrage as he slapped her, and it could really get inside Anderton's resentment of his employers and the Nazis they used to get their way. Longendyke had seen Lynch in action, negotiating with Arab terrorists for time and then hitting hard, all agreements set aside.

But, in the two and a half hours it had been sapient, it had learned pragmatism.

Now it was slumped, resting, while Lynch went about his business. The CSD man was marshalling his forces, hoping to pen the enemy in one place so he could take them out. 125 did not recognize the concept of an enemy. It knew that the crowd in the Humanities Block was, in a sense, an extension of itself. Within their bodies they harboured its viral cousins.

Only 125 could bring them the awareness of their purpose. They were a part of it, and ought to be in its thrall.

Through Lynch, it would enlarge itself. Then it would see about finding something to do with its life.

'When?' it asked.

'Soon,' snapped Lynch. 'I want the suitcase first. Then we can declare ourselves independent of UCC.'

'Very well.'

'Just think about your list of demands for Josh Unwin. Start with a billion pounds in gold. No, make that gold and voting stock. There's no reason we shouldn't come out of this with a controlling interest in this god-damned company.'

Lynch went back into a huddle with an alarmed NCO.

Someone had dug up the specs for the building, and he was formulating a siege defence scenario.

125 was at a loose end.

One of the radio people was staring at it. Most human beings found it horribly fascinating, it seemed. This was a girl. Quite a pretty one, it supposed. Anderton would have responded to her. It tried an expression that was supposed to be a smile but came out as something hungrier, more threatening.

'Hello, dollface,' it leered, 'what time do you get off?'

The woman turned away, and paid more attention to her earpiece.

125 was getting restless. It had heaps of unfulfilled potential lying around, and knew it was not getting any younger. It had to let Lynch play soldiers, but already it was impatient to have its day in court.

It could hear a noise that might be music, and someone claiming to be the Voice of the New Humanity. That amused it. The presumption. But at least there was a nascent awareness of the fact that there *was* a New Humanity. It would be ready to fill the gap soon.

Monica felt for his pulse. It was not there.

Trust Brian to run away when things were at their worst. It had always been a characteristic of his. This time, she could not blame him.

She had been crying for hours now. Not sobbing, not losing control. But her eyes were watering constantly. She did not know she had that many tears in her.

She turned Brian face up, and touched him over the heart to be sure. Nothing. It must have been a massive stroke. He was not even forty. Of course, he had been under a little extra strain recently.

Monica caught herself thinking calmly and rationally, and wondered if that – rather than Brian's grief, panic

174

and self-destructive frenzy – was the real symptom of total insanity. She was going to have to deal with the fact that most of the people she knew, most of the people she had dealt with on a day-to-day basis – liked, loved, slept with, eaten with, argued with, been bored by, negotiated with, laughed at, shared with – were dead. Or, worse, were not really people any more.

Poor Brian. And poor Jason, poor Abigail, poor Vice-Chancellor Jackson, poor Cazie. Poor, poor Monica.

Monica Flint, losing it at last.

She sat by Brian, straightening his hair. Wiping the dirt and mess off his face with a tissue.

She did not sing to herself like Ophelia, or want to throw herself under a train like Anna Karenina.

Finally, she knew she would have to live up to her responsibilities. She had been elected by the student body to take care of their interests, and they deserved her attention in this chaos. It would probably mean dying with them, but that was better than sitting here surrounded by corpses, waiting for somebody to come and kill her where she was.

Outside the next cottage but one, she could see a motorbike. A dead man – one of the trendier professors – was lying beside it, a bunch of keys in his frozen hand.

Great. She had some wheels.

Eddie Zero sliced Sam the Sham and the Pharaohs out of the rack, and lined up 'Woolly Bully' on the turntable. He cut his rap, and let the track play.

Ideas were exploding sexually out of him. He was the music, and the music was the root cause of the whole thing.

He shook his shoulders to the tune, feeling the excitement building in his gut.

Sam the Sham (Domingo Samudeo) finished his thang, and Eddie popped back, spieling fluently into the mike.

'I got this theory,' he told his listeners, 'that the music has got into our brains like a psychotropic drug, and is altering the structure of our cerebellum. It was slow at first, probably started with Elvis and Chuck Berry back before your mother was born, but it's been snowballing ever since, gathering momentum. Now, its time has come. We're the real reality. Rock 'n' roll and beat and psychedelia and punk and rap were just hiccoughs. This is the ittest of the its. It's beyond music, beyond mayhem. Just dance, mutant boppers. Dance until you drop, fuck until you faint, be until you be-bop. And here's The Pleasant Valley Boys with "EEEEE-YAH! The South's Gonna Rise Again". . .'

He had had to barricade himself in the studio, and put down some minor hassles with the collective. They were not into the way he had outvoted that cow Posie. But Stu and Sheena were with him now, and they had dealt with the whingers. Funkmaster Dee was in the waiting room, garrotted with copper wire. Sheena kept putting the calls she was getting through to him. The external lines were out, but the campus phones were still hooked up. He had a lot of listeners, was getting a lot of feedback. Everybody wanted him to stay on the air.

'Yo there, Homo superior,' he said into the phone, 'you're on the air, talk to Eddie . . .'

'H-h-hello,' said a voice. Male, young, spotty, miserable, a loser. 'Eddie, I've got a problem . . .'

'We all got a problem, space kidette.'

'. . . but I got a *real* problem. My legs don't work any more. And I think my backbone is kind of . . . jellifying? My whole body is squishy. I had to use a pencil to stab the buttons to call you up. I'm in my flat in East Slope, and I don't think I can move any more.'

'And that's your problem.'

'Y-y-yes.'

'Hell, is that all? I thought you had a real heart-breaking case of dribbly farts or something serious. You've just got to put all your old preconceptions behind you.'

'I h-h-have?'

'Yeah, chill out. You gotta learn to play the cards you get. So, you're turning anelid on yourself. Well, maybe that's the best thing you could have. Worms are herma-phrodite, you know. Are you a hermaphrodite, caller?'

'Well . . . I . . . uh, no . . .'

'Any problems in the genital area? You got a squishy sack of jello and a fish finger down there?'

'Uh . . . uh . . . uh . . .'

'You just gotta get rid of this sentimental attachment you've got to the vertebrate lifestyle, caller. So you can't walk, talk or do the turkey trot no more? Who cares, just so long as you can squirm, crawl, squiggle and slime your way. Just to cheer you up, here's Burl Ives singing "Ugly Bug Ball". . .'

The record came on, and Eddie hung up. Loser, he thought. A lot of people were not ready for this flesh trip. He was there to help them.

Eddie had grown a pair of dangling antennae that gave his greasy pompadour a 'My Favourite Martian' look. He kept brushing them back, but they just sprang up again. Bastards. He had also grown an indestructible erection, and had had to open his jeans or die.

At first, he had shafted Sheena while the records were on. She had suddenly warmed up to the idea, after all these months of no-way-no-how. He could get himself off in the three-minute playing time of the average single and still have enough breath to do the next link. But she could not keep up with him after the fourth or fifth side, and was busy with the switchboard now.

He was still ejaculating periodically. It was the rock 'n'

roll. There were strands of semen over the discarded records Posie had left on the floor.

He gripped the arms of his chair as he came again. A jet of come came out of his dick like toothpaste vigorously squeezed from a tube. He beat his own record, and splattered the far wall.

'Thanks, Burl,' he said as the song ended, 'and now here's one for those of you crying alone at home, needing a good cheering up. "Pillow Talk". . .'

Eddie could not resist giving a spin to Doris Day. Nothing was more out of line than Doris Day, but he could not help himself. He got off on it. Doris's voice got to the head of his dick better than any flesh girl he had ever known.

Jesus. His erection was an uncontrollable rod of flame.

'Hey, Stu,' he shouted at the studio manager, 'come get Posie out. It's fucking cramped in here, and she's beginning to smell good to me!'

Stu came in, and took a hold of Posie's shoulders. Eddie had just folded her up and packed her into a gap where she would go, and now she was stuck. Stu had three-inch teeth like needles and almond-shaped cat's eyes. He licked his lips with a rough tongue and he eased Posie out of the studio.

Eddie reached for the 'Easy Rider' soundtrack album, and lined up the cut he wanted to spin next. He knew who was born to be wild now . . .

Lynch met the chopper himself.

He went up on the roof. It was flat and big enough. He had had four flares set off to light up the landing area. He could not hear the helicopter coming in for the racket of Doris Day – Doris Fucking Day! – but he saw the lights from a long way off.

It was dark now, and the burning buildings near the

main entrance were sending flames fifty or sixty feet into the air. There would be fire engines soon. UCC could not stop people seeing the blaze and reaching for the phone. The place was on a main road.

The perimeter patrols had been useless for hours. Most of the infectees were in the Humanities Block, but some must have breached the boundaries and be fleeing on foot or in vehicles. Even the suitcase would probably not take 125 out completely, then. It was typical corporate stupidity, but on an unprecedented scale.

Lynch was mildly surprised that he still had so many people with him. He would have quit obeying orders hours ago, and run as well as he could. There had been some drop-outs, but they seemed to be due to infection rather than the decay of discipline. UCC trained its people well; this lot really did act like Zombies.

He could hear the helicopter now. It was fifteen feet or so above the roof, and hovering. Inside the perspex bubble, he saw two figures in what ought to be deep-sea diving suits. One waved. It had no discernible face.

The bubble opened, and a megaphone clicked on.

'Catch!'

The suitcase fell out of the air, into Lynch's arms. He clutched it. It was as heavy as any other full metal briefcase, and someone had stuck a yellow smiley patch on it.

The chopper closed its bubble, and started upwards, like . . .

. . . *like a bat out of hell!*

'Fucking bastard scumsuckers!' he shouted inaudibly into the chopper's wind.

He held the case up to his ear, like an idiot expecting an explosive device to be a ticking black cannonball with a fuse in the top and BOMB written on it. There was no sound, no hum, no nothing.

But he knew UCC had slipped him a live one.

He put the suitcase down, and pulled out his Magnum. The company's mistake had been in sending a civilian chopper, rather than one of its military models with an armoured fuel tank.

Or maybe the boardroom jockeys did not consider that revenge might be a part of his psychological profile.

One shot should do it.

He took aim at the tanks of the retreating helicopter, and pulled the trigger, feeling the recoil like a sledgehammer-blow to his wrists.

He made a neat hole, and waited a split second . . .

Clare was one of the new humans still on the roof. Most of Cazie's followers were downstairs, listening to her speechify in the School of English and American Studies lecture hall. Clare liked to be out of doors. It was good for her new complexion.

She had shed her skin entirely, but the new one was doing fine. It secreted fine oils, and she could see rainbows forming and breaking in the wrinkles at her joints. It felt like a designer wetsuit.

Her voice hissed when she heard it.

Cazie was still fond of her, and that gave Clare a certain cachet with the others. She would stay on the roof with her new friends until Cazie needed her.

They watched the man on top of the Chem Building shoot the helicopter down. It was very professional. They all applauded as he took aim like Dirty Harry, and squeezed off a single shot – which they could not hear over Steppenwolf – at the bumblebee machine. He must have holed the petrol tank, because it exploded in mid-air in a ball of orange and red. Sparks and flaming chunks rained. It was a fireworks display. The burning hulk, bent rotors sticking out of it, crashed downwards, jamming nose-first into the library steps. There, the fireball exploded in an eye-punishing burst of light and heat.

A wave of hot air struck Clare, and dried her skin out. Her glands worked overtime, squirting from her pores. She summoned a horny-handed lad to massage her. He was eager to please. She turned on her back, and pulled him down onto her. He went still and did not do anything. She tried to remember what she always said at parties to get talking to someone, then said, 'What'sssss your major?'

'Uh . . . uh,' he stammered, 'c-c-classics.'

'Interessssting?'

'N-n-not really.'

Her tongue came out, latched onto his lips, and drew him towards her mouth.

They melded by the firelight.

Clare remembered Thommy and Rote, and came like a supernova when she realized how dead they were, how much they were missing all of this fun.

It was good to be in at the start of something important.

There were still people about she could talk to. They were straggling away in small groups, mostly headed for the woods, but some just moving from place to place at random, trying to stay alive.

Monica stopped her bike and tried to get information whenever she could. From a few words exchanged with someone she had once – all of three days ago – had to interview for a part-time union post, she had a rough idea of the situation on campus.

It was Arts vs Sciences, as usual. The crazies, whom she could not help but think of as Cazie's people, were all over the Humanities Block. The Zombies, Lynch's crew, were operating out of the Chem Building. Both factions were in disarray, but both had some sort of purpose. And they were at war.

The problem was that, the way things were, Monica did not know which side to throw in with. How could she best serve the interests of the students! Or of anyone else?

Hating herself for it, she knew she would have to go with Lynch.

She kicked down, and the bike's engine revved. Wheeling across the lawns, she zig-zagged towards the Chem Building.

The machine was bigger and heavier than anything she had ridden before, and she felt sort of guilty about violating the crash helmet laws. Apart from anything else, a skid-lid might have stopped any stray bullets.

There had been a major explosion by the library, and a crowd was dancing around the fire, as if waiting to pull baked potatoes out of the ashes.

She could not get up speed because there were too many ankle-catching chain-link fences around. Most people who came off bikes wore padded leather that protected them a lot better than her sensible skirt and blouse would.

By the VG shop, a brightly coloured group from the Gay Soc were taking turns raping an unpopular member of the rugby club. None of the participants were particularly human any more. 'A try,' shrilled a high-pitched voice, 'now go for the conversion!'

The bike hit the slope that led up to the Chem Building, and she pulled back on the handlebars, leaning forwards, willing the machine to conquer gravity and get her up to the forecourt.

By the doors, where Cazie's picket line had been, there were a couple of Zombies with guns.

* * *

125 was being a bystander.

Lynch had the suitcase on a bench in the lab, and one of his men, Willis, was tapping it.

'Any ideas?' Lynch asked it.

'No. I shall be interested to see how you deal with this problem.'

'Great.'

It was intrigued by the round yellow paper face attached to the suitcase, and made an inquiry about its significance.

'Don't ask,' Lynch said.

Willis pulled out a pair of pliers and clipped something. He opened the suitcase. There were complicated works inside it, packed tightly.

'It's standard equipment,' Willis told Lynch. 'Not tricky at all.'

'Then switch it off.'

'Ah . . . but there's no off switch.'

Lynch was being very cool about it all, 125 thought.

'How long have we got?'

'Difficult to tell. There should be an LED timer showing, but they've painted over this one.'

'Thank you, Josh Unwin.'

Willis took a scalpel, and began scraping. 'There. Eight hours, twenty-three minutes, and some seconds.'

'That should be enough for Josh and the board of directors and the cabinet to get on a plane for Hawaii, right?'

'Lynch,' said 125. 'I'd appreciate it if you could deal with this fairly quickly. We have other things to do.'

'Okay, okay. Willis?'

'I can try, of course. My preferred course of action would be to get in the truck and drive like crazy, but I suspect the company will have thought of that . . .'

'Right. We're outlaws. If we leave now, they'll shoot us down. If we stay, we wind up a fine radioactive ash.'

Willis tapped something in the case. Lynch winced, to 125's amusement.

'If I can get in here, I might be able to put the timer out. That won't disarm it, of course, but it will stop it going off. In fact, it'll give us some bargaining levers.'

'How so?'

'We'll have joined the Armageddon Club.'

'What?'

'With this in our possession and under our control, we'll be a nuclear power.'

That, 125 thought, sounded interesting.

08: 09: 17

'Our enemies, the Unscrupulous Chemical Corporation and its toadying government lackeys, are in the Chem Building, sisters and brothers,' Cazie told her audience. 'We must smite them, crush them, kill them, smash them, mash them, gash them. They must be put out of our way if we are to grow as I think we know we must grow. Proliferation is what we are after now. And conversion. And transformation. We can latch onto this rotten, class-ridden, iniquitous, inhumane society and eat out its fucking heart. They used to say we were powerless, wanking around with ideals and hopes we'd jettison as soon as we graduated to the so-called Real World. Now is our chance to piss all over that. Once we've taken the Zombies out, we can spread, go into the places the Imperial High War-Bastards live and spread our loving kisses to them. We can change them, we can change society just as we have changed ourselves. We can remake the Real World. Are you ready to take what you need and do what you can? I think you are, I *know* you are. Remember, we're the new humanity, and *we've got something to say!*'

The crowd went wild. This is what it must have been

like at Woodstock, at Agincourt, at Nuremberg, at Alamogordo, at the Winter Palace, on the Long March, at Greenham Common, in London when Berlin fell.

Cazie reached out and loved them all.

08: 02: 53

Shaun Bensom had given up waiting for the bus, and started walking. It was only an hour or so to town on foot across country and through the back roads.

He hoped there was some food in the flat. After his day on the picket, he was hungry.

Nobody was about.

07: 49: 38

Monica was lucky. The Zombies did not kill her on sight.

'Lynch,' she shouted. 'I've got to see Lynch.'

They lowered their guns, and let her into the building. It was hard to be heard through the hoods, but she managed to make herself understood, and an officer scuttled off to find the big man.

She stood with a single guard, a faceless figure with a camouflage poncho over its whites. Besides its hood, it had a tin hat and khaki knee-protection pads. It was a miracle the person inside could stand up and walk, let alone fight a battle.

She did what she usually did when she had to stand about waiting in some corner of the University, and read the notices pinned up on the board. The announcements of plays, concerts, exam timetables and lectures were surreal after what she had been through. She found it easier to deal with the reality of armed guards in decontamination suits and familiar faces turned monstrous than with the forgotten rut of normality.

The officer returned, and signalled for her to follow.

He led her upstairs, into what had been the common room.

It was Hell. In the middle of the room squatted a monstrosity the like of which was even beyond Monica's recently traumatized and expanded powers of credulity. It was big and wet and parts of it were horribly familiar. It had faces, and hands. And other organs she had not thought to see on the outside of anything alive. It churned, and bugged out several of its eyes at her.

'Hello,' it said, 'I love you, won't you tell me your name . . .'

'Don't mind that,' Lynch said. 'It's only 125. There are more pressing problems, Ms Flint, as I'm sure you appreciate.'

'Wha . . . wha . . .?'

'Hiya, cutie,' the thing said. 'Grab a chair and get yourself some coffee. *Ave Maria*, gee it's good to see ya!'

Lynch took her elbow and steered her past the thing.

'You'll get used to it,' he said. 'Now, what's your problem?'

'I came because I . . . I don't really know. I . . . we have to do something. To help these people.'

'We're trying. There are complications I don't want to go into at the moment. Where's the guy you were with?'

'Uh . . . dead, I guess.'

'There's a lot of that about. Did he get it?'

'It?'

'The bug. 125.'

'Maybe. I think he just died. You know, died.'

'Have you got any symptoms?'

'No. I . . . uh . . . don't think so.'

'No physical alterations? Peculiar mental quirks? Strange sexual urges?'

'It's difficult to think straight. I've overdosed on the unusual.'

'That sounds like ordinary combat fatigue to me. You're probably okay.'

Monica felt lightheaded, but could not remember her train of thought. She felt sleepy, wanted to drop off.

'She's immune, Lynch,' said the thing. 'Like you. A lot of people can't get me, you know. Anderton never bothered to say that. Maybe 25 to 35% of you have no chance of ever coming down with me. I'm not AIDS or anything special.'

'But why are all these people listening to that crazy bitch in Humanities?'

'Mass hysteria. It's not my fault. You've been shooting down healthy people all afternoon, probably. After all this is over, we'll talk disease vectors and communicability and immunology and work it all out. We might even get a grant.'

Monica had caught something in Lynch's talk with the thing.

'Crazy bitch?'

'We've picked her up on the internal bugs we dropped earlier. Cazie Bruckner. You know her?'

'Christ, yes.'

'Well, she's the Typhoid Mary of this whole thing. She thinks she's Queen of the Mutants, and is firing up her horde to come over here and storm the palace. Which is okay, since we're ready to defend this place.'

'Good Lord!'

'Yeah, but we can handle her. You won't believe this, but she's only the second most dangerous thing we have to deal with in the next seven and a bit hours.'

The thing scat-sang 'My ba-ba-bayby loves BANG-BANG!'

Lynch turned on it, and shouted. 'Fuck you, 125! Get a grip on that brain tissue you're cultivating in there. It's running wild, going to fucking pot. If you crack up, our deal is off, you hear, *off*! I'll fry you in napalm, sterilize

187

the stain with super-strength Domestos and seed the field we lay you out in with salt. Knowing you, you'll live, but you won't think and talk and bloody whistle "Dixie" any more! You'll be just another bug, and we fucking wiped the floor with scarlet fever you know, and bubonic plague! They were much tougher than you too! 100% susceptibility! 10% fatality. None of this pissing around. We got them!'

'What about cancer, creepo?'

'It's not a virus!'

'Neither am I, any more!'

'Then just what the fuck are you in there in that disgusting mess of an excuse for a body, 125?'

Monica could have sworn the thing smirked with all its mouths.

'I'm what you're afraid of, Lynch. What you think I am, but don't dare say out loud. I'm a fucking *monster*!'

It reared up and waved its arms and roared like a pride of lions. Teeth shone in its gaping holes. Then it sat back, and chortled like a dirty-minded little boy, fixing its gaze on Lynch, then Monica, then Lynch again.

'So,' it said, 'go about your business, and call me when you need me.'

Monica was aghast, tired of disbelieving everything she saw.

'Lynch,' she shouted, 'you made a *deal* with that! What did you sell us out for? What kind of a fucking ratscum human being are you?'

He looked at her. She remembered how scary his eyes were. They fairly gleamed with unhealthy light. His facial scars were red lines, filled with angry blood. His voice was calm now, his outburst of anger spent and gone.

He answered her question. 'Ms Flint, I'm a monster too.'

* * *

07: 38: 10

Captain-Equivalent Lawrence Fairisle Willis peeled back the aluminium covering, and looked into the workings of the clock. Very clever. Solid state circuitry set in a lucite block. He would have to chisel and melt his way in there to take the mechanism out.

07: 31: 01

He reflected that it was a good thing nuclear fission was tricky. If he was dealing with a conventional explosive, he would have to watch out for double-bind tripwires. Here, there was only one way to set off the bang, and once the clock was out of the system, it would be as safe as any suitcase with a plutonium payload.

07: 22: 43

Willis heated a scalpel over a bunsen burner, and sank it into the lucite like a hot knife into butter. He scooped a glob out and scraped it on the bench.

07: 11: 52

The red numbers counted down.

07: 03: 00

07: 02: 59

07: 02: 58

07: 02: 57

He had had to swallow a lot today. It was a good thing he was being well paid for this. He wondered if UCC would compensate his wife if the suitcase went off. They would probably fight it in the international courts. UCC were like that. He wished he had set up his own firm, got into high-level security. There was always a demand, and the rewards were great. But he just liked the company pension plan, and the protection. He had never realized how little he mattered to the decision-makers. Even Lynch was a tax write-off when it came to the crunch.

06: 56: 23

So far, he had had combat, rioting students, some sort of plague, nuclear weapons, revolt in the ranks, Dionysiac orgies, rock 'n' roll, teenage werewolves and fifteen-foot-high monsters out of H.P. Lovecraft. He wanted to take a rest from this late, late show plotting.

06: 42: 45

At least he knew what he was doing.

06: 38: 05

He lifted another glob of melted lucite out on the scalpel, and raised it to his mouth. He scooped it with his tongue, relished the burning heat for a moment, and swallowed.

06: 34: 18

At least. He knew. What he was. Doing.

06: 30: 53

Snip.

06: 29: 16

Oops, there goes a wire. He had meant to leave that until later. No harm done, though.

06: 28: 49

At Least. Knew He. Doing. What Was.

06: 28: 17

He kept on eating the lucite. It did not taste of much. But it was filling. He could not feel anything in his mouth anyway. He had to be careful not to cut himself with his scalpel.

06: 12: 38

The red numbers kept pestering him. He wished they would just go away and let him alone.

06: 08: 37

Bastard red numbers.

06: 01: 09

06: 01: 08

06: 01: 07

06: 01: 06

06: 01: 05

06: 01: 04

06: 01: 03

06: 01: 02
06: 01: 01
06: 01: 00
06: 00: 59
06: 00: 58

He scraped and scraped. He might have cut a few more wires he did not mean to, but that was no problem, at least . . .

05: 58: 52

What. He. Doing. Knowing. What Was. Him.

05: 58: 51

At least . . .

05: 58: 50

Clare had new eyelids under her old ones. They opened sideways. Now, it was not night any more. She would have to think of names for the new colours. She did not know there could be new colours, but here they were. Not red or pink or green or orange or purple or blue. New.

Her new boyfriend was called Michael, and he was awfully nice. He had the buds of horns on his forehead, and his limbs were short and strong. They were compatible. She would never have to push him through a floor.

When Michael was not looking, she slid off the ring Thommy had given her for her birthday and swallowed it.

She would shit it out later and have done with it.

'C'mon everybody,' said Eddie Zero over the P.A. 'Don't be a spaz, go with Caz! Get your footsies over to the H block, and be with the crowd that's loud. There's a lady there who'll fuse your shoes, and here, just for her, is "Killer Queen" from the sounds of the '70s . . .'

Clare knew Cazie would soon have enough people with her to do the job properly. Last time, they had fucked up badly. Now, they would take the Chem Building properly, and trash the whole monument to exploitation and Evil.

This was what she had got into the Movement for.

05: 46:19

On the forecourt of the Chem Building, Lynch's men had set up a couple of light field machine guns. And Monica saw Zombies waddling in heavy grey suits, toting flamethrowers.

'You can't just kill them,' she told Lynch, aware of how stupid she would sound to him.

'You got a better way?'

'There's still something left. Even the worst of them have minds. You should be able to reach them.'

'Horsecrap, Ms Flint. Those people are gone forever. Dead. We're just disposing of the detritus. According to 125, it's mostly fatal. No matter how active the bastards are, tomorrow they'll be dead. This is a lot quicker and kinder than letting the bug take its course.'

'But . . .'

'Have you seen the ones who melt? Or the ones who sprout too many new organs and turn inside out? There are eight million stories in Viral City.'

From all over the campus, she could hear rapid spurts of gunfire, shouts, chants, the ringing of fire alarms.

All this noise must be carrying. People would notice. UCC could not get another team in to seal off the whole area immediately, no matter how they hurried. This was going to spread.

Stragglers were still coming in. Men from Lynch's perimeter details who had somehow got through the carnage, immunes seeking protection from the crazies. A couple of field medical people were checking them over for symptoms.

She left Lynch to set up his defences, and joined the

medical crew. One was from Lynch's outfit, the others were University people. The people coming in were being put in the main lecture hall. Most of them just sat quietly, and watched the lectern as if there was a talk on. If there was an opposite to mass hysteria – mass catatonia? – this was it.

There were armed men in the hall. Just in case.

The checkpoint was just a desk. Monica stood by, while a brusque nurse processed the latest arrivals. She shone a pencil light in a girl's eyes, then looked at her hands, felt for her pulse, and stroked her face with mechanical tenderness. She nodded, and the girl was taken into the hall to join the others.

Next up was an elderly man, one of the catering staff. He passed too. But then came a young Asian in a tracksuit. He flinched when the nurse shone her torch in his eyes, and made a grab for her. Two men had him before he could connect. Monica could see his eyes were wrong.

He was snarling and howling like a wild beast, hitting out with the squash racket he had refused to give up his hold on. The men – not Lynch's people, but campus leftovers, Monica thought – dragged the infectee off, down a corridor, and into a supply room.

'What . . .?' Monica began to ask the nurse, but she was busy on the next arrival, a sobbing, middle-aged woman.

A shot echoed, and the two men came back to their posts.

'How many?' Monica asked.

The nurse shook her head, and went on with her work.

05: 17: 48
Gold and Hopkins had been in a lay-by with a couple of

mugs of thermos tea and the latest issue of *Knave* when the first of the calls came in.

Gold turned the centrespread of Jackie from Slough on its side, and then upside down, so her face was the right way up.

'Wish you were real, darling,' he murmured, slurping hot tea.

'Pervo bastard,' said Hopkins.

'Garn! Look at them nipples. Big as top hats.'

Then the radio came on, and the report of a disturbance at the University got through to them.

'. . . Local residents have been calling in with fairy stories about riots and shooting. Also, fires. The brigade is on their way out. Take a look will you, Zebra Golf Tango. And hit some students for me.'

'Wilco, out, we'll get the rubber hoses,' Hopkins chuckled.

Gold put Jackie from Slough away, and started driving the police car.

'I thought we were off the campus since this morning, since those London boys came in? Woolbridge pulled us out.'

'The London boys probably started the riots,' Hopkins said. 'It'd be just like them to send in some superhard patrol group to deal with a pissy drugs break-in. Now, we'll have to haul their little botties out of the firing line. As usual. Ouch, drive carefully, I've spilled my tea.'

'What about the fires?'

'Oh, some student gets pissed as a fart and breaks the glass on the alarms every bloody week. Saturday night, usually. We had a place in town – dry-cleaning shop – burned to the ground last year because every engine in the place was crawling around the campus looking for a fire. Old McKendrick's crew just like the idea of pulling a lot of student bints out of their beds in the wee small hours.'

'Naked, most of them? Or in those flimsy nighties?'

'Pervo bastard.'

It was not a long drive, and they found the fire engines blocking the main entrance. There was even a real fire. The big buildings by the car park were practically blazing rubble by now, and no one seemed to be doing anything about pissing them out.

Gold wondered about the plain trucks in the car park. They did not look like the usual things you saw on the campus.

'Where are those brigade bozos?' Hopkins shouted at no one in particular.

'Should we call in for assistance?'

'Want the Professionals to come and hold your hand, boy?'

'No, but . . .'

'Listen, you sit in the car. I'll go scare up some people and find out what's happening. I'll see if I can get some tea anywhere.'

'Reg, I'm not sure I like . . .'

'Sissyboy pooftah.'

There was someone standing in the headlight beams, a tall figure in a long yellow coat like the fishermen wore, with a helmet on. Lit from beneath, Harry McKendrick's face looked like a horror movie maniac's. He held his hands out in a stop signal.

'Harry, you cretin,' Hopkins said as he walked towards the fire chief, 'why aren't you deploying your forces properly?'

Gold saw a two-shot of Hopkins and McKendrick in the Panavision windscreen. The fireman loomed over Reg like King Kong. His face was streaked with soot, and he was soaked. Gold could not hear what Reg was saying to the man, but he could see that McKendrick was not answering him. There were others in the dark, shambling shapes that gathered around the fire chief.

195

McKendrick's arm went up, into the darkness beyond the headlights' throw, and came down again. Hopkins staggered and fell onto the bonnet of the police car. A red smear appeared high up on the windshield.

Hopkins's checker-circled cap was pinned to his skull by a fireman's axe. He pulled at the handle, and then stopped moving. The splash across the window was an irregular graffiti splurge now. Gold could not see much past it. He reached for the wipers button, but felt stupid and sick.

He had not made up his mind what to do when the doors were pulled off the car and the hands came in for him.

'Bloody copper,' he heard a voice yell, 'get his balls!'

04: 45: 22

125 had almost lost interest by the time the word came in that the enemy was coming.

It was sorting out bits and pieces of knowledge, memory and impulse taken from its former personalities, and subsuming them into its viral identity. It was a learning experience. It was amused by the mutual feelings that Anderton and Finch had never been able to share, and reflected that their lives might have ended differently had they extended their relationship outside the laboratory. Still, they were together now. Longendyke was still there, if only as a trace element. The jittery addict was like a foul taste 125 could not lick out of its mouths.

It did a little thinking about its plans for the future. There was a notion of biological destiny it found quite appealing. It was curious to see whether it would be absorbed by the human race or vice versa. One thing was certain, a new dominant lifeform would rule the world once this struggle was over. Whatever emerged from the battle would be unrecognizable to the old world.

Lynch interrupted its train of thought with the news.

'The mob is on its way, 125. If you come over to the window, you'll get a good view.'

There was a crowd approaching. 125 could see it a lot better than Lynch, because of its altered eyes. The flaming torches the students carried, like peasants from a '30s Frankenstein movie, burned splodges into its retinae. It beheld its children, and was fairly pleased with them.

Lynch was excited. 125 could tell he enjoyed the prospect of a battle.

'I'll be back,' he said, and left.

The first shots were fired, from snipers on the roof, and people in the crowd went down. The dead did not fall. They were carried on by inertia, pinned between shoulders, finally dragged under by some obstacle catching a foot. As many of the living were trampled.

There was a girl in there who 125 was interested in meeting.

It still had no direct experience of Cazie, but it had been keeping up with the reports. She might well be the first human to come to terms completely with the 125 in her system. The girl could be one of the triumphs of the symbiosis. That made her important. It hoped Lynch would refrain from killing her.

It felt a species of pride in its offspring, and recognized in the emotion an echo of Anderton's suppressed feelings for it. Human relationships did not go in circles, but in bramble-tangles.

The first wave broke, and fell back, leaving dead or wounded people on the forecourt. Some of them had deviated considerably from the human pattern.

The crowd regrouped, and surged forward again.

04: 08: 52

Monica had to be in the battle. She could have huddled

with the shellshocked victims in the lecture hall until it was all over and one side or the other came in to exterminate them, but it was not enough. She had to see this through.

Perhaps she would even get killed, and not have to worry any more.

The front hall was full of Lynch's men, piling out to join in the shooting. They dipped into cases of ammunition as they passed the reception desk, and jammed clips into their guns. Monica noticed that the last few men had to take only one clip apiece.

Lynch had not mentioned it, but she guessed they were low on firepower. They could not have brought much ammunition with them. This thing had developed far too quickly to be well thought-out by anyone.

That gave Cazie's crowd a good chance of coming out on top. Only to be vaporized in a few hours by UCC's suitcase.

Terrific.

Lynch was on the steps outside, barking orders, firing off short bursts from the hip. The monster was not in sight.

Monica slipped through the doors and went out.

It was as bright as day. Fire rained down from the flamethrowers. There were burning people everywhere. The field machine guns chattered and shook on their tripods for almost thirty seconds, and were silent. They had only one belt of ammunition apiece. Lousy organization. But, within range of the guns, lay a wedge of dead and dying.

The fallen were fantastical creatures, barely recognizable as the transformed human beings they were. Monica saw faces like starfish, scales and plumage, talons and pincers, huge eyes and mouths. There, in the front rank, still bleeding a clear, watery fluid, was Lindy

Styles, half her face swollen and fungoid, the other half normal.

God.

The last time she had seen Lindy, she had been rounding up student volunteers to partner Lynch's perimeter patrols. Now, she was a mutant and dead.

Monica hugged herself, and tried to keep back.

A line of flame passed over the bodies, and they caught instantly. Lynch was directing his flamethrower people to create a barrier of the burning dead.

The stench hit Monica's nose.

A Zombie near her freaked out. The smoke had grimed his faceplate, and he could not see. He waved his arms, and blundered into the flames. His suit must be fire-resistant because he kept flailing about – a black figure amid the white-hot blaze – for minutes.

She could not hear anything. It was so loud, she was inured to it all. Once, at a rock festival, her ears had felt like this. That had lasted for weeks afterwards.

Then the fires went down, and the students started coming through.

Three figures plunged through the curtains of flame, and twitched in the gunfire before falling in smouldering heaps on the forecourt. Then another two, then more. They came, and they died.

A girl, her long braids going like roman candles, got close enough to a Zombie to rip through his suit with her bare claws. She died, but Lynch's men shot down her intended victim along with her.

They were losing already.

03: 39: 10

Willis's mouth was a blackened ruin. Most of his tongue was gone, and his palate was patched with drying lucite.

But he was still hungry.

199

03: 27: 46

He had already eaten all the foam rubber packing, and crunched up a couple of circuit boards. The jacketing he had skimmed off the electrical wiring was easy to chew and swallow, but some of the metal components hurt when they went down.

03: 19: 16

The red numbers were still flickering, but he would have them stopped soon.

03: 16: 28

He had tried to bite through the metal cylinder in the middle of the suitcase, but had broken a few teeth for his pains. He had picked up the shards of enamel and gulped them back without trying to taste them. He knew he was dribbling blood.

03: 09: 17

Really, all this was just an appetizer.

03: 01: 04

He was very, very hungry. And he had heard that plutonium was supposed to be delicious.

02: 57: 18

125 was spreading. It kept its bulk in the common room, where Carole Ricci and the rest of Lynch's communications people were doing their best to ignore it as they co-ordinated the fighting, but it extended itself into the ventilation system and the interstices between the floors. It probed the extremities of the Chem Building, sucking in a great deal of electrical wiring. It was running a little short of living material to counterbalance the huge quantities of inanimate matter it was using to fortify itself. 125 would need some more human flesh.

It found a few corpses within reach, and snaked tubes to them. Those that had been dead the longest were just meat, but two still had flickers remaining in their brains.

125 nurtured and cherished the new information, even as he redistributed the bones and organs.

Eyes were especially useful.

02: 37: 19

Lynch could feel the tide turning. He knew his military history. Everyone remembered the 300 Spartans, and Davy Crockett at the Alamo, and Custer at Little Big Horn, but nobody admitted that those people had lost the battles. Their achievement was holding out as long as they did while ridiculously outnumbered, but they had still got killed at the end.

That was what would happen here. He had started with maybe 150 people. The enemy were in their thousands. He had the guns, but could not keep them operational.

And the bastards he was fighting did not care whether they lived or died. That made them dangerous.

He was already considering withdrawal scenarios. And he had 125, if the monster could pull through and if he could trust it.

Fucking monster!

He looked at his watch, and tried not to think of Willis.

02: 26: 49

Cazie was immortal, invincible, God-only wise . . .

. . . but she knew enough to be at the back end of the horde as they stormed the Chem Building. Her newborns would have to soften the Zombies before she could take part in the victory.

Her hair was standing on end now. Electricity whip-lashed as she walked.

She had lieutenants up front, directing the attack. They could execute her designs faithfully. She still thought up the strategies, and gave instructions, but she knew how to delegate authority.

'You'll bow before me, UCC cocksuckers!' she yelled, 'and then we'll see what's what!'

She had picked her personal troop carefully. None of the melters, leakers, bleeders. None of the half-formed, those trapped between stages of humanity, dying like fish in acid. Only the best, the most perfect, the most adapted of the new humanity were selected for her private cadre, her elite guard.

Elliott Frazier stood by her side, her official bodyguard.

She watched the battle, watched wave after wave disappear through the now-feeble wall of flame. There was less gunfire now. Good. The weapons would soon be gone, and old humanity would have only its weak and useless hands and limbs to fight with. Then she would step forward to inaugurate the new era with a mass spilling of the blood of the old.

The fire chief was with the cadre too, unable to talk because of the tigerfangs crowding his mouth, but as alert as a big cat on the prowl. He had grown out of his uniform as his body changed, but still wore his yellow poncho and red helmet. A tall man before, his elongated, hunched back made him a giant. When the fire brigade had arrived, and the spark of growth had leaped into the chief, Cazie had seen a way into the Chem Building. She was thinking faster now, down multiple trains of thought, foreseeing, calculating, planning . . .

There was another spurting of fire from the UCC flamethrowers, and the barrier sprang up again. Another packed-in mass of Cazie's followers was consumed instantly. Some scattered like fireflies, but most stood their ground, pressing forward.

There were only single shots now.

Cazie extended her fingers, and sparks leaped and danced like Tinkerbell. The fire chief smiled ferally, and raised his hand to catch the blue light. An arc coursed between them.

'Now,' she said.

The fire chief nodded, and swung himself gracefully up into the seat of his vast, beastlike machine. Cazie's corps, already aboard the fire engine, cheered, and rattled their weapons in salute.

Elliott Frazier buzzed his arms, now huge and heavy with chainsaw elephantiasis, in the air, and the shreds of his jacket at his shoulders were agitated, spitting out chunks of stranded cotton.

Eddie Zero sang through his bullhorn, accompanying his ghetto-blaster, one of the old songs. 'Johnny B. Goode'. He was out of the studio now, but still on the air.

Cazie climbed up into the broad seat beside the fire chief, and lazily gestured.

Lightning ripped the air, and the vehicle rolled forward.

02: 02: 37

'Funny how people get off on killing other people, isn't it?' mused 125.

'Pardon?' said Ricci.

'Nothing really.'

'Fine.'

The woman went back to talking into her throat microphone. 125 had the idea that the battle would not go well for the CSD. They were highly trained and facing a rabble, but sometimes random unpredictability was an advantage.

125 was intrigued by the line of Ricci's throat, the tiny pearl-like studs in her earlobes, the trace of a perfume she must have tried to scrub away before hitting the field.

There was a lot of activity outside, still. 125 could see the bright red fire engine driving up, crushing bollards, and ripping up grass like a bulldozer. A crowd swarmed along beside it, shouting and chanting. Firing rapidly, the outermost guards were falling back to the Chem Building.

125 was wondering whether it had dealt with the right person. If Cazie Bruckner took out Lynch, it would have to renegotiate with her.

At least they had something in common.

01: 49: 16

A stream of water, as solid as a concrete girder, shafted through the fire, knocked men and guns out of the way, and broke against the side of the Chem Building.

Monica was out of the line, but still got soaked. The jet cascaded off the wall, and the forecourt was awash.

Another stream came, tearing up tiles, and churning brown clouds of dirt. A Zombie was caught by the water, and lost his arm cleanly to the high-pressure jet.

Windows shattered, and frames were pulverized.

The fire wall was going out.

Then the juggernaut came, rolling over the charred bodies of its slaves, blaring Chuck Berry, bearing the inheritors of the earth.

Monica saw Cazie in the fire engine, and marvelled at the change in the girl.

A few shots went off, and a cobweb crack appeared in the engine's broad windscreen. There was answering fire from some of the things perched up on the half-raised ladder.

Lynch was waving his arms. His shouts were lost in the din, but Monica knew what his signal meant.

Fall back.

A suited figure grabbed her arm, and pulled her back with him, into the lobby of the Chem Building.

She could not understand. It took her a moment to

realize the Zombie was looking out for her, saving her life.

The gesture did not mean as much as it would have done yesterday.

Her saviour slipped on the wet floor of the lobby, and sprawled, skidding backwards. The fire engine mounted the low steps, and crashed into the front of the building. The doomed man burst under its front wheels.

Monica ran with the rest, as bricks parted and glass fragmented. The front cab of the engine rammed its way through the double doors, and the head of the beast was caught inside the building.

Lynch personally fired off a burst at the windscreen, which became as white and opaque as packed sugar, then fell away entirely.

In the cabin, a figure danced and jerked as Lynch killed it. Ropes of blood squirted out through the broken side windows.

It was not Cazie. It was a fireman.

Cazie was gone.

There was noise upstairs.

'Fuck,' shouted Lynch. 'They're inside!'

01: 25: 51
Flesh petals were blossoming from the holes in Clare's side. She had been shot a couple of times, but that did not hurt at all.

She zig-zagged down the corridor, running with the others. If anyone got in their way, they were knocked down and trampled. Someone usually took the trouble to kill them. Clare did not have to do that sort of thing any more.

Elliott Frazier strode behind the first wave, finishing people off with a rasping pat on the head. He only had to touch his whirring club hands to a Zombie's mask to turn the white headshape into a red ruin, shot through with shards of glass and bone.

Last term, Elliott Frazier had given her a C+ in the Modern European Mind course.

Clare's insides were growing faster than her skin, swelling up her stomach, clogging her breathing. Her new skin was splitting, and she saw raw redness in the cracks.

Already, she was dragging an armful of internal organs around with her.

Whatever it was she had had, she was losing it now.

Finally, she just stopped running and curled up on the floor to wait for it.

It did not take long.

Death settled on her like a black bat, wings folding around her head, darkness blotting out her eyes.

00: 54: 17

Lynch was nearly down to his bare hands, which put him easily on a par with the enemy.

On the stairs, he caught a hunched over goat-thing and broke its back with a practised move.

Whoever was left ought to be retreating to the common room. That would be the last ditch.

Shit, this was a crazy way to die!

He wondered how Willis was doing, and rather hoped he would just fuck up, cut the wrong wire, and bring down instant oblivion.

Like the UCC people thought, it would tidy things up.

He stepped in something that had been a girl amphibian, its guts already hanging out of great tears in its abdomen. Noxious fumes farted out of the corpse.

Lots of the enemy were being laid low like that. 125 had said it was mostly fatal.

If he was doing this all over again, he would have

grilled the monster more, found out more about the fucking bug.

Someone big and dangerous with frizzed hair and tusks came out of an office, and he wasted it with his last bullet. He got rid of his last gun, and ran towards the common room.

What a life!

00: 48: 05

Cazie was calm and confident. There must be only a handful of the Zombies left, and her people were everywhere.

Her elite clustered around her protectively, keeping the jostling rankers away from her spark.

Clare was dead with honour. But Elliott Frazier was still with the programme.

They came down from the upper floors, swarming in through the ladders that had breached the windows of the big laboratories. They met little resistance.

Still, a lot of her people were in bad shape. One or two had just upped and died for no reason at all. Evidently, only the strongest could take being hiked up the evolutionary scale.

'Cazie,' someone growled, 'look!'

It was Eddie Zero. He had found a small hatch, leading to a projection booth. Through the aperture, Cazie saw the main science lecture hall. It was full . . .

. . . full of . . .

'Food,' said Eddie.

'Later,' she snapped, 'later.'

Back in the corridor, someone was waiting for her, a cockatoo-plumed woman she had picked for the elite earlier.

'Where are they?' Cazie asked.

'The common room. There aren't many.'

Cazie was serene. She felt the thrill of winning, but wanted a moment of peace.

It passed.

'Okay, let's finish this thing.'

00: 32: 51

125 saw how the fight was going. From its remote eyes, it saw the students prevailing against the CSD forces.

Now, the battle was inside the Chem Building. Inside its body.

It took its flesh where it could be found, reabsorbing itself from the systems of many of the fallen. New consciousnesses crowded in, granting new insight, offering new sensations.

Many of the new components had been significantly mutated by their earlier exposure to 125, and it was pleased at the new shapes and forms they had found.

It suspected that its effects on human beings had a great deal to do with individual psychology. 125 made whims flesh, reshaping bodies to fit unconscious minds.

It took a particular type of mind to become perfect.

125 regretted Lynch's immunity. After Cazie, he would have made the ideal avatar.

It draped itself stickily across corridors like a curtain, entrapping those who blundered into it.

With each component it absorbed, it became better, stronger, smarter, more fit . . .

00: 29: 18

Monica collapsed on a chair in the common room. She guessed the Zombies were down to single figures.

She had a stitch. Momentarily, she thought she had been shot, but there was no wound.

She gasped for breath.

The monster was up and about, swaying on its spiny legs. It would be a shock even for Cazie, Monica thought. It had grown, and it seemed to be fixed to the walls and ceiling like a complicated appliance, organic plugs slotted into holes. Its tentacular appendages pulsed like snakes swallowing large rats, and lumps were funnelled into its main bulk.

God, she wished she could have this day over again. She would stay in bed, or emigrate to Australia, or go home to her parents, or any bloody thing . . .

Lynch had blood on his hands. At least she supposed it was blood. He stood with the monster, tensed and ready.

There was nothing for it but to wait for Cazie.

00: 27: 27

Eddie went through the swing doors first, then came out again dead, a knife sunk to the hilt in his face between his antennae.

That gave Cazie some pause, but her aides swept past her and into the common room. Eddie was mashed underfoot.

Cazie stepped forward, and went into the room.

Shit! Fuck! Jesus!

What was *that*?

'Hello, Ms Bruckner,' it said.

00: 25: 52

No one moved. 125 was in control.

It tipped itself forward, and looked at Cazie Bruckner. A halo of blue flames seemed to shimmer around her head, but she was in deep shock.

'You don't know me, but you've got me, so to speak. I'm Batch 125, your disease. Your symbiote, to use the word of the day. Actually, I'm not all that symbiotic, as you'd have noticed if you had paid attention to the way ninety-three out of a hundred of your fellow infectees self-destruct within a few hours. Congratulations. You're one of the very few people who have been able to come to terms with having me.'

She was obviously smitten at first sight. Her blue aura flushed red, and, mouth agape in wonder, she came forward, her hand out to touch 125. She was extraordinarily beautiful by anyone's standards. At least, certainly by the standards of all the people whose brains 125 had absorbed. He felt he had taken enough grey matter on board to make his own aesthetic judgements now.

He opened a mouth and wolf-whistled.

The girl got close to it. Lynch stepped between them.

'We've got a deal, 125!'

125 shot a few quills at the CSD man.

00: 18: 26

Lynch took the darts in his neck and shoulder. A rush of excruciating pain shot through his entire body.

A barbed arm came out of 125's bulk, and stuck into his chest. He felt the triple claw sink in, and heard his ribs crack.

He was lifted off the floor.

This would teach him even to consider trusting a fucking virus!

He kicked, his combat boots scraping carpet.

His bowels let go.

125 was talking to him, but he could not listen.

The charge hit him through the hooks in his chest. With the first jolt, he went into convulsions. He twisted badly enough to break his spine.

125 had developed some sort of biological laser, and was shocking him like an electric eel.

His brain fried. His eyes popped. His skeleton burned

white hot, and turned to ash in his body. He was cooked through in seconds.

00: 16: 07

Monica held her nose.

125 dropped Lynch through the hole in the floor. He stuck in the gap, speared by upward-bent rods.

He had died with his eyes open.

125 roared with something that might have been laughter. Cazie was slowly sinking to her knees, ready to worship the creature.

Infectees were crowding into the room.

Elliott Frazier – the dreamboat TV prof – took aside one of Lynch's surviving soldiers and took him apart with a few swipes of his whirring, swollen, bloody arms.

Somebody tried to surrender, and Elliott did for them.

Lynch's last radio operator took off her headset and carefully put it down. Nobody bothered her.

Monica kept looking back at Lynch's black, bloodied face. She did not know whether she should envy the dead.

Now what?

0: 08: 19

Willis picked up the clippers, snipped the final wire, and . . .

. . .

00: 08: 18

. . .

. . . the little red numbers stopped.

00: 08: 18

Cazie sat down, and watched the monster pick through the leftovers.

All but three or four of her cadre were dead or dying,

and the monster was sucking out bits and pieces, incorporating them into its already-vast bulk.

Elliott Frazier submitted to it. He offered up his arms, and they were sucked into the doughy lump of the monster's body. He looked back one last time, smiling slightly, and let the wave of flesh engulf him, sucking him in completely. A wall of warty skin formed behind him. She heard his distinctive buzzing, muffled by the ton of flesh, and the skinwall undulated in agitation.

She wondered if it had thought how it would get out of the building. It was already bigger than any of the doors. The only hole big enough for it was jammed up by the fire engine.

It did not seem to bear her any malice. She thought it might be rather fond of her. It extruded a head on an arm, and kissed her on the mouth with it.

A charge coursed through her body.

The head was hairless, but had Elliott Frazier's handsome face.

She was almost satisfied.

125 dangled tendrils into the laboratory, and reached for Willis's head.

The delicate filaments went into the man's brain. It was riddled with virus, but 125 could pick up the information it needed.

The suitcase was out of commission.

125 let Willis go. There was no point in killing the man and, after all, he was probably the only human being who would ever – intentionally or not – save its life.

It had Cazie under its spell already, and that gave it all the cards.

It was a shame the human body really was not a very good vehicle. It was susceptible, but too fragile to keep the virus alive in its system for more than a few days. 125

was beginning to realize that it was not the super-virulent plague it had been sold as.

There were infectees spreading out there, passing on the disease. But without the concentrated exposure the original victims had had, the next generation of infectees would struggle on, and maybe even fight off the virus. A few steps down the line, and it would be no more serious than a cold.

Under natural conditions, it could just have mutated into another anonymous disease and never have been more than a footnote.

But it had this body, which was adapting very nicely to its purpose. It was the smartest bug that had ever lived.

And it had Cazie Bruckner.

Monica watched the thing grow.

Already, it was more like a plant than an animal. Its flesh clung to the walls, and grew into the ducts and out of the windows. Arms and legs hung semi-uselessly from its branches, a nasty reminder of its raw materials. Eyes peered out of pink masses. Elliott Frazier's head surveyed the room, a familiarly thoughtful expression on its face. If 125 could find a wig and a pipe, it would be able to do a perfect impression of the professor.

She thought it was probably all through the building by now. There had been an appalling wail earlier, and the thing had been very active. Then it went quiet, and the flesh reddened. New blood. It must have got into the lecture hall. There would have been more than enough flesh in there to feed the creature, but probably not enough to kill its hunger. Hundreds more were dead, but she was too tired to feel stricken by the loss.

She tried to remember faces. There had been a crowd in the hall, sitting quietly, waiting for rescue. But they seemed less real than the individuals, than Brian, Jason,

Lindy, Frazier. Even than Lynch. She would never be able to watch anyone pretend to die in a war film or a Western again without remembering.

It looked for a while as if the thing would eat Cazie, even. It was talking very quietly with her, almost seductively. Then, it wrapped the girl in tendrils of flesh. Cazie was lifted off the floor, held in a writhing web of tissue. Her face was serene, almost beatific. The flesh folded around her, nuzzling her like a kitten. Only her head was outside the creature. Then, Cazie gasped, and her body wriggled within its sleeping-bag-like cocoon. With acute distaste, Monica realized the creature was making love to its high priestess.

That completed her day.

Cazie felt 125's touch all over her, and felt its extruded flesh slipping into her body, warming her loins, moving gently, pumping into her. There was an electrical crackle as they joined, and she was having another of her minute-long orgasms.

Her brain danced, and dreams flickered behind her eyelids.

125 was her ultimate father-lover.

For several months when she was five or six, her father had taken to coming to the nursery and touching her private places. She had repressed the memory, but realized how it had formed her.

125's touch washed away the stain Daddy had left.

Cazie did not now know what her father had meant. She thought his touch had been innocent not exploratory. He could not have been thinking of anything else.

125's voice was inside her, encouraging her, passing on what it had learned, seeking out new pleasures for her.

She changed her mind about her name. There was nothing wrong with Corinne.

214

She hung in the webbing of its flesh, her legs braced, her insteps arched as 125 grew inside her, teasing, pushing, secreting.

It loved her without question.

That made it unique in her life. She felt wetness on her face, and realized she was crying.

When it was over, 125 allowed Cazie to slip out whole again. What was left of her clothes was gone, as was her pubic hair. She had been licked clean and dry.

She looked like an alien Eve, her body sparkling where 125 had caressed.

Monica was not able to look at her.

Cazie slept now, under its protection. For the first time, she saw the girl completely relaxed.

It was still eating everything. Monica guessed it was taking minerals aboard as well as living matter. Its hide had metallic patches, and some parts of it were a bricky orange.

She wondered why she had been left alone. Too insignificant to be a problem, she supposed. Not like Lynch, who had long been squeezed through the hole in the floor and eaten up. There were others alive in its coils, she knew. Lynch's radio operator was sitting still on her chair on the other side of the room, apparently untouched and untouchable.

It was nearly morning.

125 had completely annexed the Chem Building, making it a part of its body. It would need to be a giant to survive among human beings. A giant of flesh and steel and concrete.

It had absorbed over a thousand brains, and learned many things, many skills. Most of the personalities it had snuffed out quickly, but it was sampling the range of human character types. It even absorbed Frank Lynch,

215

taking on board his grasp of strategy and his lack of regard for human life. It was beginning to get a good idea of what the world beyond the valley was like.

It knew that people were going to be its biggest problem. It had to eat more of them, to know more about them. It had to be big enough to be indestructible, and smart enough to avoid capture and enslavement. But, through the minds it was starting to think of as its ancestors, its contributors, it had read millions of books, lived through countless situations – wars, love affairs, divorces, seminars, rock concerts, crimes, riots, orgies, demonstrations, political meetings, films, plays, murders, arguments, jokes, reconciliations, deaths, births, illnesses, childhoods, injuries, triumphs. It was developing an all-round personality.

It ate people, it ate walls, it ate furniture, it ate girders, it ate stone, it ate plastics. It went through laboratories indiscriminately, absorbing chemicals, elements, whatever. There was little it could not use somehow.

It would stay where it was for the moment, and solve the problem of mobility later. It suspected that it could detach parts of itself and send them out to do some of the more fiddly jobs on their own. It could convert many of the dead people at its disposal into puppet creatures, linked to it through strong, thin filaments. Perhaps, in time, it would learn to be smaller.

It would keep Cazie, and a few others, inside, near its brain. It wanted external input, and someone to talk to.

It sucked the building's electrical works into its system, and distributed the wiring throughout its body, snaking the plastic-and-rubber coated strands alongside its veins and nerves, then growing solid sheathing around all three systems. It detached itself from the mains, remembering through several different consciousnesses the 1950s science fiction film in which the vegetable monster is electrocuted. It knew lots about a lot of things.

It had eaten a movie buff somewhere along the line. The film was *The Thing From Another World*, 1951, directed by Christian W. Nyby, produced by Howard Hawks, based on the story 'Who Goes There?' by John W. Campbell, Jr, and starring Kenneth Tobey, Douglas Spencer, Margaret Sheridan, Robert Cornthwaite and James Arness as the Monster.

Knowledge filled up the back of its brain, the random accumulations of several thousand lifetimes systematically sorted out and put to use. 125 felt that it could sing, kill, make love, cook, change a fuse, repair a car, write an opera, type, solve a crossword puzzle, follow the plot of *EastEnders*, educate a child, handle a hostage crisis, do a million other things.

To replace the mains, it generated electricity and amused itself by keeping on the lights in the common room. It concentrated hard, and was able to do it, although a sudden surge popped all the bulbs along the ground floor corridors when it first began to generate.

Then it ate something that disagreed with it.

'Noooooooo,' screamed Willis, 'it's mine! Mine!'

The obscene tentacles that had grown throughout the laboratory fastened on the suitcase, and cut through the metal casing of the core as if it were an eggshell.

'My plutonium! My ploot! Mine! Mine! Mine!'

The suitcase disappeared entirely into the main sucker.

Willis chewed a wooden bench in frustration.

He filled his mouth, and found himself stuck into the bench, held fast by his growing rows of teeth.

His heart and lungs stopped minutes after his mind had gone.

* * *

As soon as it tasted the radioactive material, 125 realized it had made a mistake. Tendrils of death shot out like cancers from the ruptured suitcase, leaving dead tissue in their wake.

125 tried to retreat, but the death grew, looking for its consciousness.

The weight of useless flesh began to drag it down. It felt itself coming apart, fragmenting.

The plutonium pumped more death into it.

Whole areas of its mind went dark as the black crab fed on its brain. Death ate and absorbed it as it had eaten and absorbed its components.

It rediscovered pain.

Like Lynch, it resolved to fight to the end. As death encircled it, 125 vowed to survive.

It tried shedding large lumps of itself, rending away live sections to prevent the plutonium poisoning spreading just as houses had been blown up to block the Great Fire of London.

It did no good. The death was in its system now, in its blood. It could not be rid of the poison.

There were so many things 125 wished it had done . . .

Monica woke up to find 125 in a bad way. Chunks of it had fallen off, and lay congealed and greyish on the carpet. It hung loose from the ceiling and walls. The lights were off.

'Overextended yourself, didn't you?'

It did not talk back.

Cazie was still asleep, curled up like a kitten. The radio woman was still sitting, calm and mad.

Monica got up, and left the common room. The corridor was full of the stink of death. Withered and shrunken rows of flesh hung like party ribbons. Dead bodies grew out of the mass.

218

125 was dead or dying. She knew it was not a miracle. She knew the virus was just an organism like her, and the world was a hostile place. It had made a mistake in thinking itself invulnerable, not that she could blame it for reaching the conclusion.

She went downstairs. There were holes in the walls, and oddments of debris littered the main hall. 125 was kicking weakly in some places, but mostly it just hung and putrefied, slimy lumps falling off.

She squeezed past the crumpled fire engine, and came out into a bright summer day that hurt her eyes.

The campus was quiet. It looked like a WWI battlefield. Most people in sight were dead. Water was still dribbling from the firehoses. A few fires persisted. Early birds had descended, and were picking at the corpses, tearing loose bite-size chunks. A few other survivors were wandering around dazed, or slumped asleep with dew on their faces.

125 had extended itself beyond the building, squeezing thick, leathery tentacles through the sewage outlets and other holes in the wall. They hung, life dribbling away, human features liquefying. A snapping dog was tearing at one mass of the creature, shredding through olive skin to the pink meat beneath.

She sat down on the damp concrete forecourt, and crossed her legs, and cried.

Somewhere, overhead, helicopter blades sliced the air. They got louder.

EPILOGUE

Reason in the Age of Lunacy

Corinne had been strapped down for weeks now. The leather thongs at her wrists and ankles were reinforced with half-inch-thick metal bars, and a wide steel belt held her midriff to the iron cot which, in turn, was bolted to the floor.

They had been feeding her intravenously, and doing tests. She was fed up with tests.

From one of the nurses, she had gathered she was not the only one in the facility. There had been other survivors. Some of them had died in the early days, but she knew she was not in danger.

The voice in her head told her she would survive.

The nurses were all pretty and pleasant, and definitely not working for the National Health. One of the doctors had said something about 'the corporation' picking up the bill, and so she supposed she was being held by UCC.

In a sense, she appreciated the rest.

They had opened her up and looked around and sewn her back together. They had X-rayed her from every conceivable angle.

The voice in her head told her she would be strong.

Once, early on, she had got her fingers to a nurse, but now they watched her hands, and kept her nails clipped. They had to do that every morning with industrial pliers. It hurt, but Corinne did not scream and shout any more.

The voice in her head advised her to keep quiet and calm, to wait for her time. It would be soon.

This could not last.

No one had come to visit her in hospital. She supposed her parents thought she was dead.

Actually, if Josh Unwin were personally to telephone her father and inform him that he was holding prisoner and torturing Little Corinne, Daddy would probably go along with it. Daddy was a big fan of Josh Unwin, and would not let go by a chance to lick the bigger fish's bottom clean. No matter what it cost.

She would be a better parent. They had not told her yet, but she knew already.

It was the voice that talked to her inside her head.

She had been getting her strength back. She knew she could break restraint any time she wanted. But for the moment she lay back and took her food in the arm, and pretended the shots they gave her had some effect. They were stupid.

They thought they could get rid of it, but were dithering. She would be out before they ever came to a decision.

She knew lots of things they did not.

Like, for instance, she knew who the father was.

THE QUORUM

Coming soon in Pocket Books, the stunning new novel
by **KIM NEWMAN**

**'Brilliant … tantalising, Newman's prose is a
delight, his attention to detail spellbinding'** *Time Out*

With friends like these who needs enemies?

The supernatural and social satire mix equally in this
dazzling relocation of the Faust legend to contemporary
London. As the plot sweeps across the last thirty years,
Kim Newman brilliantly captures the mood of each
decade: from the swinging Sixties to the materialism of
the Eighties. Now, in the Nineties, the era of having it
all has had its day and the devil has come for his dues.
And as *The Quorum* so icily demonstrates, there really
are fates worse than death.

'The best thing he has done yet … totally gripping'
Lisa Tuttle

'Kim Newman's prose is a pleasure to read' *Sunday
Telegraph*

Published 7 November 1994
POCKET BOOKS
Fiction
ISBN: 0 671 85242 6
PRICE: £4.99

Also available by Kim Newman
0 671 71591 7 **ANNO DRACULA**
0 671 71562 3 **THE ORIGINAL DOCTOR SHADE
& OTHER STORIES**

THE QUORUM   0-671-85242-6

These books are available at your bookshop, or can be ordered direct from the publisher. Just fill in the form below.

Price and availability subject to change without notice.

SIMON & SCHUSTER CASH SALES,
PO BOX 11, Falmouth, Cornwall TR 10 9EN

Please send cheque or postal order for the value of the book/s, and add the following for postage and packing:

UK including BFPO - £1.00 for one book, plus 50p for the secound book, and 30p for each additional book ordered upto a £3.00 minimum.

OVERSEAS INCLUDING EIRE - £2.00 for the first book, plus £1.00 for the secound book, and 50p for each additional book orderd. OR please debit this amount for my visa/ Access/Mastercard (delete as approporiate)

CARD NUMBER ....

AMOUNT £ .... EXPIRAY DATE ....

SIGNED ....

NAME ....

ADDRESS...